# KETURAH AND LORD DEATH

Martine Leavitt

FRONT STREET

*Asheville, North Carolina*

LIBRARY OF CONGRESS CATALOGING-IN-PUBLICATION DATA
Leavitt, Martine.
Keturah and Lord Death / Martine Leavitt.—1st ed.
p. cm.
Summary: When sixteen-year-old Keturah follows a legendary hart into
Lord Temsland's forest she becomes lost, and eventually Lord Death
comes to claim her, but when she is able to charm him with her story,
she gains a reprieve of twenty-four hours, if she can find her one true love.
ISBN-13: 978-1-932425-29-1 (hardcover : alk. paper)
[1. Death—Fiction. 2. Interpersonal relations—Fiction.
3. Love—Fiction. 4. Grandmothers—Fiction.] I. Title.
PZ7.L4656Ke 2006
[Fic]—dc22
2006000799

FRONT STREET
An Imprint of Boyds Mills Press, Inc.
A Highlights Company

815 Church Street
Honesdale, Pennsylvania 18431

*For my dear girlfriends,*
*who have blessed and enriched my life*

*Because I could not stop for Death,*
*He kindly stopped for me;*
*The carriage held but just ourselves*
*And Immortality.*

—from "The Chariot" by Emily Dickinson (1830–1886)

Keturah and Lord Death

# PROLOGUE

"Keturah, tell us a story," said Naomi, "one of your tales of faërie or magic."

"Yes, Keturah, do," said Beatrice, "but I would have a tale of love."

The boys around the common fire groaned. "A story, yes," said Tobias, "but a hunting tale, please, one of daring and death."

The men murmured in agreement. One, whose face I could not see, said, "Tell a tale of the great hart of the lord's forest."

Choirmaster sighed. "I would prefer a godly story," he said, "one to comfort your heart on a gloomy day."

The fire crackled and leapt for a time, and then I said, "I will tell you a story that is all of those things, a story of magic and love, of daring and death, and one to comfort your heart. It will be the truest story I have ever told. Now listen, and tell me if it is not so."

# I

*Of myself, Keturah Reeve, and the personage
I meet, a story scarce credible to one who
has never been lost in the woods.*

I was sixteen years old the day I was lost in the forest, sixteen the day I met my death.

I was picking new peas in our garden, which is bordered by the forest, when the famed hart, the hart that had eluded Lord Temsland and his finest hunters many times, the hart about which I had told many a story, came to nibble on our lettuces. I saw that he was a sixth-year hart at least, and I would have run at the sight of his antlers, spread like a young tree, had I not been entranced by his beauty. He raised his head, and for a long moment he looked upon me as if I had stumbled upon him in his own domain, so proud he was, and so royal. At last he slowly turned and walked back into the forest.

I meant only to peek into the trees to see more of him. I thought only to follow the pig path a little way into the forest in hopes that I might have a new story to tell of him at the common fire. I thought I saw him between the trees, and then I did not, and then I did, and after a good long while I turned about and realized I was lost in the wood.

I walked a deer-trod that wove its way for a time along a

ridge above a ravine. Far down in the cut I could hear water, a creek, but I could not see it. The way was too steep. Trees grew upward out of the sheer face of the ravine. Some had fallen and lay like blackened bones in the clutches of the upright trees.

I left the path in hopes of finding an easier way to the creek, but soon I could no longer hear the water at all, and I could not find the path again. Still I walked.

Trees, which had once seemed benign and beautiful to me, blocked the sun, fell before my path, tore at my hair, and yielded no fruit but bitter leaves. When night fell, I slept at times, and each time I dreamt that the forest went on forever.

After three days of wandering, I reconciled myself to God and sat under a tree waiting for death. I thought sorrowfully upon Grandmother, who would be weeping by the window. I thought upon my dreams that would never be realized: to have my own little cottage to clean, my own wee baby to hold, and most of all, one true love to be my husband.

I slept and woke at intervals in my upright position against the tree, wishing dearly that I might not have to spend another night in the dark wood. I had not enough water in me to make tears, but my heart wept with longing to see Grandmother and Gretta and Beatrice and my beloved Tide-by-Rood.

At dusk, death came to me in the form of a man.

He was dressed in a black cape and came mounted on a black stallion. Beneath his hood I could see that he was a goodly man, severe but beautiful, not old but in the time of his greatest powers. My courage failed me. I wanted to escape, but I was too weak to stand. My limbs seemed rooted in the ground beneath me. The tree I leaned against cradled my shoulders.

I remembered the good manners Grandmother had taught me with her switch and paddle. When he had dismounted and was coming toward me I said, "Good Sir Death, forgive me if I do not rise."

His steps slowed. "You know who I am, then?"

"I do, sir."

The dusk deepened, as if the gloom unfurled from the folds of his cloak.

"Is it Keturah?" he asked. His voice was calm and cold, and thrilled me with fear. "You are the daughter of Catherine Reeve, whom I know."

"Yes, sir." He knew my mother indeed, but I did not. She had died giving birth to me. "I regret to say, sir, that, as in the case of my mother, you have come before I was ready."

"No one is ready."

"Forgive me, sir," I said, without hope, "but there was something I wanted to do."

"Your doing is past." He hunkered down on one knee as if to get a good look at me. I saw that where his boot had been, the grass was utterly crushed and flattened. "You were foolish to come so far into the wood."

I did not look in his face but studied instead his powerful thigh and his great, black-gloved hands.

"I followed the hart, sir, the one Lord Temsland tries

to hunt, the same hart who last winter led his herd to raze the lord's haystack." Somehow the sound of my own story voice comforted me. "Tobias said the hart once fought off a wolf—"

"Silence," he said.

It was not harts or wolves that would save me. I looked for worms about him, but he was clean as stone, as far from life as wind and rain and cold. Perhaps there was no story that Death had not already heard. I felt my eyes begin to close.

"My lord, I have not slept for cold and hunger and insects these three nights," I said. "Will I sleep now?"

He stood. "Do you try to be brave? It does not sway me," he said, prouder than a king.

That was not what I had intended, but I replied, "I am brave, sir. I have had much practice. I was born into death, my grandmother has told me many times. It filled my mouth upon my first breath. I sucked it in, Grandmother says, and cried as if my heart were broken, and even my dead mother's pap would not console me. My father searched you out to find my mother and died before my first tooth, so that it became my grandparents' burden to raise me. Then my grandfather died after I had lived long enough to love him. I have been in conversation with you perhaps all my life."

Now his pale, severe face softened. "You have grown to be beautiful and honest, too, Keturah," he said, "for all you have said is true. How old are you?"

"I am sixteen, sir," I said. A beetle crawled on my hand, but I had not the strength or heart to brush it away.

"Sixteen—many younger have come."

He reached forward. I held my breath, but he only brushed the beetle away from my hand. I could scarce feel his touch but for the coldness of it. I met his gaze. His face was craggy but noble, as if it were cut out of fine stone.

"If I chose a bride," he said, "she would have your courage."

What would it be, I thought in a moment of terror, to be the bride of Death?

"Sir," I said, "I cannot marry you. I—I am too young." A feeble excuse, since many in my village married at a younger age.

He appeared startled. Then he laughed, a frigid, haughty laugh. " 'Twas no proposal but only a compliment."

If I had not been so weak, I would have blushed for shame.

Then he said, "You *are* too young to marry, Keturah. And too young to die." He put his hands on his hips, and his cloak billowed in a breeze I could not feel. "Therefore, I will give you a boon: choose whom you will to die in your place so that you may live."

"You mean that someone else . . . ?"

"Only name the soul, and it shall be," he said. His voice had become stern again, and lordly. It echoed in the wood. "Choose."

I thought of my poor, shabby village, nestled in the farthest corner of the kingdom, and my heart longed for it. How dear it seemed to me, and how dear all in it.

"No, sir," I said. "I cannot."

"Your grandmother is old," he said. "I will be coming for her soon anyway. I say it will be her, for she is even now praying that her life be taken instead of yours."

"I decline your offer, sir," I said, trembling, "for I love her dearly, and the life you gave me would be too bleak without her."

"No one declines me."

"But I do, sir."

His dark eyes seemed less cold then—a great relief to me—and I thought perhaps those might not be the last words I ever spoke.

Lord Death said, "Choirmaster, then? All he wants, I understand, is to sing in heavenly choirs. This I could arrange. Surely it is not long before he mourns himself into the grave."

I shook my head. "Sir Death, if you heard him play the organ, you would know why it cannot be him. Even his saddest music makes a cloudy day one to be glad for, and a sunny day one of joy."

"What of Tailor?" His gaze left me and lifted—toward the village, I suspected. "Though half of him lives for his children, the other half of him longs for death so he might see his wife again. He will come soon to me anyway."

"But his children need him, sir, for as long as they can have him."

"The village gossip, then. She causes nothing but trouble," he said.

"She makes everyone feel better, for she can always tell you of one who is worse off than yourself. Please, not her."

"There are many old in the village."

"Sir, each is loved by someone young, someone whose heart would break. Besides, the old are full of sin and may need one more day to repent."

"There are many very young who have no sins at all. I could make it quick and painless. Pick anyone—it makes no difference."

I gasped. "I would die three deaths before . . ." I swallowed the dust in my throat. "No, sir, it shall have to be me."

"I tell you, your courage is to no avail. Many of them will die anyway, much sooner than you think."

"Sir, what do you mean?"

"Plague comes," he said.

Plague!

"And those who live," he continued, "will wish they had died, so great will be their sorrows."

Plague. *Plague!* The word clanged in my brain like a bell.

"I—I will tell them to flee," I gasped. Around the common fire I had heard tales of the plague, so horrible I scarce believed them.

"The swiftest horse cannot outrun the plague," Lord Death said, and though he said it without pity, he also said it without joy.

"When does it come? And whence?" I pressed.

Lord Death did not answer.

"Tell me—tell me how to stop it!"

"Even if you lived, it is not in your power to stop it.

Your manored lord, perhaps—but it may be too late even for his efforts. Lord Temsland has allowed his lands to fall to dire ruin."

I did not know how that had anything to do with the plague, but I could not ask him. A sob must escape my mouth if I spoke.

"But you could be spared," he said.

It was as if I had awakened from a three-day sleep. My mind was a whirlwind, and at its center was a single word, black and quiet: plague. I knew I must live a little while, if only to warn my village.

Then he removed his black gloves without taking his shadowed eyes from me. "You don't mind if you die."

"Oh, yes, sir, I do!"

"Of course you do. What is it, then, that you want to live for, Keturah Reeve?"

My heart nearly broke with sadness, for I realized I had lost feeling in my arms and legs and that the life was indeed going out of me.

"My desire was that I might have my own little cottage to clean, and my own wee baby to hold, and most of all, one true love to be my husband."

He was unmoved. "That is not too much to ask of life," he said, "but you must have none of them, since you will not choose someone else to die in your place." He put his cold hand on my head. It felt heavy, as if it were made of lead instead of flesh. I felt lighter after he released his touch.

"Have you killed me?" I asked.

"No," he said. "You are still alive. For now."

"Why did you touch me?"

"It is not for you to question me," he said.

He had spoken truly—I was very much alive. I heard the birds of the forest singing more clearly than I ever had. Had I never before noticed the pepper-musk scent of fallen leaves and bracken? No, I was not ready to die.

Nor could I bear to think of plague in my village. If only I could speak for but a little time with Lord Temsland, to warn him.

"Sir, please let me say goodbye to my grandmother."

"To say goodbye is everyone's wish at the end," he said, "but never granted. It is time, Keturah."

He held out his hand. My mind whirled, desperate for a way to live, knowing I could not run away. I could see myself reflected in his shiny black boots, my face pale and bug-bitten.

And then into my mind came a memory of Hatti Pennyworth's son, who was dragged by a horse and should have died, but lived. And Jershun South, who went to sleep for two weeks and awoke one day as if he'd slept but a night. And what about my own cousin, who once ate a mushroom that killed big men? Though he was young, he survived. Death often sadly surprised us, but sometimes he gladly surprised us, too.

"Sir, you are not easy to entreat."

"I am not entreated at all."

"But I hear you are sometimes cheated."

He laughed then, and I saw that he was perilously beautiful, at once terrifying and irresistible.

"Good Sir Death," I said too loudly, "I would tell you a story—a story of love, a love that could not be conquered even by you."

"Truly?" he asked. "I have seen many loves, and none were so great I could not divide them."

"This is a story of a beautiful young maiden, who, though she was a peasant, fell in love with the lord of the manor."

"I have heard this tale before, in a thousand different ways," he said.

"But my tale, Lord Death, is one that will make even you love, that will heat even your frozen heart." My boldness astonished me, but I stood to lose nothing.

"Indeed," said he in disbelief. "Then say on."

"Once there was a girl—"

"An auspicious beginning."

"—who loved . . . no one."

"A love story in which there is no love—you have caught my attention now," said Lord Death.

"Though her mother died giving birth to her, and though her father followed his wife to the grave soon after, the girl had been raised on love."

"I see you have given me a part in the story," said Lord Death, and if I could trust myself, I might have thought that he said it with a hint of sadness.

"The girl grew with love in the very air she breathed," I continued. "When her grandparents sat together and Grandmother was not spinning, the couple held hands. They talked together of all the big and small things of life and rarely disagreed. When they did, it became a thing of laughter. Sometimes they shared sadness, especially when they thought of their daughter, who had not lived to hold her own child.

"They danced together at village dances; they prayed together at night before they slept, and then slept close. Often, for no reason, Grandfather would bring his wife a flower. Grandmother in her garden would bring the biggest, reddest strawberry for her husband, the darkest and sweetest raspberries, the newest carrots. She made rosewater from dying roses and splashed it on herself for the sake of Grandfather. They drew the girl into their circle of uncommon love and established in her forever a desire to have such a thing for herself someday.

"After this, the girl longed for a love that could not be ended by death. From the time she was young, she knew that her true love was there, somewhere, living a life that would one day intersect her own. Knowing this made every day full of sweet possibility. Knowing that her true love lived and breathed and went about his day under her same sun made her fears vanish, her sorrows small, and her hopes high. Though she did not yet know his face, the color of his eyes, still she knew him better than anyone else knew him, knew his hopes and dreams, what made him laugh and cry."

I paused to look at Lord Death. He was regarding me with an unreadable look, a look of great concentration. Had I not seen this same look across the flames of the common fire when I told fairy tales to the villagers?

He leaned back as if to pull himself out of the web of my story. With a gesture of his hand he said, "Every girl dreams of such love. Then they marry and quarrel, and the cares of life drive love out."

"The girl knew that quarrels would come because their lives were intertwined—how passionately one defends a heart that is vulnerable," I said.

"The girl and her true love will get old and ugly." Was his tone defiant? Or was it that he wished—demanded—that I persuade him?

"They will, and yet they will see past the scars of time to view the soul that first loved."

"Could such a love be?" Lord Death asked, but his voice was not harsh.

"We will never know, for one day Death came for the girl. She knew that her soul's heart would love as much as her living heart, and that she would long and ache and mourn for eternity for her true love. She tried to persuade Lord Death, tried to make him see how dark and lonely would be the life of her future love without her. She tried to tell Lord Death how even he would rejoice for the sweetness of that hoped-for love, if only he would let it be." I was weeping now, for a truer story I had never told. "Death would not be persuaded, for he had found her first, and yet . . ."

"And yet?" Lord Death said quietly.

"The end of the story I cannot tell."

"Cannot tell?"

"Will not tell—until tomorrow. Let me live, sir," I begged, "and I will tell you the ending tomorrow."

The leaves in the trees shushed me. A wind caught some dust and leaves and swirled them into the air. The horse shied and quivered. Lord Death was utterly still. His face went from disbelief to astonishment.

"Are you saying you will not tell me?"

"Take me home, and I swear that I will come to you in the wood and tell you the rest of the story. Only let me live another day."

The wind blew his hair and his cloak, and even the shadows around him boiled. "You think too highly of love," he said. "Love is no more than a story spun out of dust and dreams, having no substance. But I would know the end, and I confess I hope you can indeed show me a love that is greater than death. Return to me tomorrow, and you will come with me then."

He smiled to himself, and the shadows of the forest clotted around him.

"And I grant you a further boon—find this love in the day I have given you, and you will live and not come with me at all. Now I will set you upon my horse and return you to your grandmother, but only until the morrow."

"You are not angry with me for being more clever than you?"

"In fact—"

He stepped toward me, knelt again on one knee, and reached his ungloved hand as if to put his hand under my chin. I raised it away from his touch. He did not lift his hand to touch me, nor did he lower it. I could feel the cold emanating from his fingers, so cold it burned into my throat.

"—I have decided that when I take you tomorrow, I will indeed make you my bride. What do you say to that, Keturah Reeve?"

What would it be like, to be Lord Death's consort? Not to rest in the world where the dead are, now and always without fear, but ever to cross from one world to another, always able to see the life that was left behind. Worse, to serve at his side in his office as the bearer of pain and tears and heartache. To see every day a man weep like a baby himself over his lost little one. To see a new widow stare at her living children with hollow eyes, her heart torn out of her. To stand at the bedside, invisible in the shadows, while great men rocked in their beds with pain. To be the bringer of plague. Ah, 'twas one thing to die, another to be Goodwife Death.

"No, sir, though I thank you. But as I said before, I will not be your bride."

Another wind gusted in the trees. The branches thrashed overhead, and a flock of black birds rose as one from the trees and flew away. The horse whinnied and shook his silver harness.

"I have decided," Lord Death said icily.

"No, sir," I said again, for I was feeling strong now. "I will not marry you. I will live and breathe and dance and tell my children stories. I will marry for love."

A moment more, I thought, and I would stand on my own legs again. I sounded brave and sure, but I confess my heart was sick and afraid, and emptier than my stomach. Plague. Plague. The wind moaned and the trees bowed low.

"There is no refusing, Keturah," he said.

His horse pawed the ground.

"Sir, then I must obey you, but I need not love you," I said. "And think of eternity with a wife who does not love you."

He lifted me as if I weighed no more than a baby, and set me on his horse.

The horse was swift, and there could be no escape. Lord Death did not speak to me, nor I to him, but my heart raged: No! I will not have you! Though you drag me into your wormy realms I will not have you.

When at last we came to the edge of the wood, where I could see my grandmother weeping through the window of our cottage, he set me down. "Tomorrow night," he said, "when the shadow of the forest touches your cottage."

"I will find my true love, sir, and I will rob you of my soul. And all the souls you would reap in the plague, too."

"Keturah," he said, tilting his head, and he turned his horse and galloped away.

# II

*In which I am welcomed home
with reservations and theories, and in which
I consider bachelors.*

Lord Death had deposited me close to the edge of the forest. I could see our cottage clearing through the trees, and Tide-by-Rood beyond.

I wobbled on my legs a moment, but I was afraid to take a step toward the cottage, thinking I might fall and never get up again. I looked longingly at Tide-by-Rood through the edging of trees.

Tide-by-Rood was the poorest village in the poorest corner of the kingdom, yet this moment I doubted there was a dearer sight in all creation. The village square at the bottom of the hill was a muddy morass, as it usually was, except in winter when the mud froze and in summer when it dried hard as a brick kiln. The cottages were in need of patching, and none more than my own. The thatch on every roof was thin and bore nests for mice and birds. The mill was an eyesore, and more than one goodwife had seen rats as she waited for her grain to be ground into flour. The boats that bobbed in the bay were tattered and gray as flotsam.

"Grandmother!" I called. When no answer came I took

a step, and fall I did. It took all my powers to push myself to a sitting position. "Grandmother!" I called again. "It's me, Keturah!"

Then came the sound of crashing through the trees. I thought it might be the great hart, and then I knew it was no wild beast but a horse. Lord Death had changed his mind, I guessed, and had returned for me.

But the horse was a golden mare, and the rider was none other than John Temsland, son of Lord Temsland, master of the lands of Tide-by-Rood.

He dismounted, took my face in his hands, and then proffered me his waterskin.

"By all saints," he said as I drank, "we've been searching for you for three days. We thought you were dead."

I wiped my mouth and chin. "I shall quickly be dead if I am left here, sir, for I cannot walk."

Gently he lifted me, and carried me. Once out of the forest, he set me upon my legs and held me around my shoulders.

"It is most kind of you, sir," I said, flustered to think that the first time the handsome young lord saw me should be after I had been lost in the forest. And then I remembered my last words to Lord Death. "Sir, I must speak with you about an urgent matter."

"First you must rest from your ordeal, Mistress Reeve, and restore the color to those comely cheeks," he said kindly.

A compliment so significant as that could not be borne by legs as weak as mine, and they folded under me once again. Young John caught me and carried me into the cottage.

Our cottage was bursting with people, all weeping and speaking in low tones.

John set me down but kept his arm round me to steady me.

The weeping and murmuring stopped.

"I'm home," I said, and my eyes lit upon a meat pie sitting atop the cupboard.

Everyone became very still, turning only their heads to look at me. All at once a woman screamed, a man cursed, and the rest drew in breath as one. Grandmother cried my name and ran toward me, arms outstretched, but Mother By-the-Way blocked her.

"Don't touch her," she said. "She is a ghost."

Grandmother put her hands on her bosom. "Are you a ghost, Keturah?"

How beautiful she looked to me, and yet my gaze fell upon the meat pie again.

"Nonsense," John said, "but she shall be if she doesn't eat that pie immediately." He helped me to the bench at the table, and Grandmother pushed past Mother By-the-Way and placed the pie before me. Before she had time to cut it, I dug into it with a spoon and ate as fast as I could.

"No ghost eats like that," Grandmother said happily. She kissed the top of my head and sat across the table from me, beaming with relief and concern.

"Where did you find her?" Gossip asked.

"Where we'd searched a dozen times—near the edge of the forest, behind her own house," John answered.

"Leave it to young John to find the girl," said one of the men.

"That's our John," agreed another, and others joined in and added their own praises.

John seemed uncomfortable with the praise and excused himself. "I will come again to assure myself that you are well," he said to me.

"Thank you, sir," I said, swallowing my mouthful of pie. "I am well enough, I think, but I would be grateful for the chance to speak with you on the other matter as soon as possible."

He inclined his head in assent and left.

How handsome he had grown to be, I reflected, with his hair the color of harvest-time wheat and his eyes green as bay water. All the villagers loved him and were proud that he could kick a ball farther than any of the other boys, and drag a boulder farther in the harness, too.

When he was gone, the guests whispered together and stared at me with long faces. They were disappointed, of course, having come for a funeral gathering. Some of the men, who'd been good friends with Grandfather when he was alive, had told stories of the forest and of all the people they'd known who had been killed by its treachery. Now, at intervals, one or another would look up at me and shake his head in wonderment, as if I had defied all the wisdom of great age.

Gossip was obviously disappointed when I appeared whole and alive, but when others began to look sidelong at me and whisper of fairies, she cheered up.

Grandmother's gaggle of friends, who had been there to cluck and clean and comfort, had brought bread and meats to make a funeral meal, even if there was no body to mourn over. Now they grudgingly turned the food into a celebratory meal.

Relatives were there, too, and more came as the news spread of my return—cousins and second cousins and great-aunts and a step-uncle. I wondered where my friends Gretta and Beatrice were. Most of all, I wondered where my true love was, whoever he might be, and if he was among my mourners.

Ben Marshall, a man of marriageable age who had of late made an effort to speak to me at doings, smiled at me. Though I had at times ventured to return his attentions, I had had reservations. He was tall and toothsome, but he had a great love of food, and already one could see signs of future portliness in him.

My deepest reservations had to do, however, with a long Marshall tradition.

Marshalls were known for their prizewinning gardens. Generations ago, a Marshall had decided that he would marry the woman who was chosen Best Cook of the village, regardless of his feelings for her, and vowed that his sons would do the same. His sons obeyed, and theirs, and now it was a long tradition of which they were inordinately proud.

The best gardens and the Best Cook in one household meant that their tables were the envy of Lord Temsland's lands, but it was well known that Marshall children were nursed on business, not love, and I, I would have love. Still,

I encouraged my hopes that I could have both Ben's garden and his heart for my very own, and that he might be my true love. Perhaps my new reputation as the one who had been stolen by fairies would be overshadowed by my reputation as the one who cooked the best pies in Tide-by-Rood.

Also in the house was Tailor. I thought of what Lord Death had said about him half sorrowing unto death, and my heart went out to him. He was a bonny man, a well-off widower something older than me, close-mouthed and pragmatic. I did not know him, really, but I knew his beautiful children. I knew that Gretta admired him for his famed and perfect stitches, and I determined then and there that Gretta was the one who could cheer his heart and make it live.

There was Choirmaster, too, perhaps the richest bachelor in the village, but God had given him so many gifts in music that there had been none left for his face. Worse, he played only gloomy music and seemed afraid of girls. Still, I had never seen him be unkind, and I wished that Death knew him not so well. I knew that Beatrice admired him; perhaps I could persuade her to comfort his heart.

There was Tobias, Gretta's brother, but he was a year younger than I, and still a dog boy who cared more about horses than about girls. There was Locky Jones, who was hopelessly cystic in the face, and one of Soor Lily's great sons, who loved only their mother. And . . .

"Keturah, are you missing the fairies?" It was Tailor's little daughter. The crowded room fell suddenly silent.

"There are no fairies in the wood, Naomi," I said, "only trees and beasts and bugs that bite."

Everyone whispered among themselves. Naomi said, "Even though you are bug-bitten, Keturah, you are still beautiful."

I gathered her into my arms. "'Tis a curse, child," I said, thinking of Lord Death.

"But how did you get lost, Keturah?" she asked, the first one to do so.

"I followed the hart into the wood, Naomi."

"She followed the hart, she followed the hart," the others whispered.

One of the older men nodded knowingly. He spoke to me. "I have heard that the deer and the forest beasts are of the kingdom of the fairies. Don't all the tales tell it? Speak true now, Keturah. Did you see the fairy king?"

With my mouth full of meat pie again, I said, "Not a fairy king, sir, nor a common fairy neither."

"And yet the hart lured you."

"Forgive me, sir, but he did not lure. It was my own curiosity that made me follow him."

The man shrugged his shoulders as if to say he did not believe me, and it was clear from the way all eyes turned away that they did not believe me either, preferring the stories I had told of the hart around the common fire. "Well," the man said, "there's something devilish and sly about the beast, and it is not just for the sake of winter hay that I say he must be hunted down."

These words brought me no happiness. The great hart loomed in my memory—tall and proud and fearless. I thought his beauty something I would be willing to sacrifice a haystack for, though lack of hay meant a hungry winter for both people and stock alike. The men's talk became louder, and soon a group was dispatched to the manor to solicit Lord Temsland about the matter.

I could taste the three days' staleness in the meat pie, suddenly. The crust was gritty between my teeth, the meat greasy and gristly. I winced to swallow and put down my spoon.

Just then, Gretta and Beatrice burst into the cottage and threw their arms about me. "We could not summon an appetite to eat at your funeral, but when we heard you had been found . . . ," Beatrice said.

"Thank goodness and mercy that young Sir John did not give up," said Gretta.

I hugged one and then the other: Beatrice, with the voice and face of an angel, who saw the good in everyone and everything and met life with good cheer, and Gretta, whose hair was always perfectly coifed, whose clothes were perfectly clean and pressed, and whose loyalty and love were perfectly constant. They kissed me, each on either side of my face.

"Eat, eat," said Gretta, sitting beside me.

"How beautifully pale you are," said Beatrice, sitting on the other side of me.

While my friends and I talked, the villagers continued to whisper, and one by one they departed. Grandmother gathered the leftovers to take to Hermit Gregor, who lived poor. When all had gone, Beatrice said, "Undoubtedly they will hereafter cross themselves every time they see you."

"I care not a bit what the villagers say," I replied. "Not a speck, not a whit, not a jot, not a tittle. My only care is to wed my true love."

Gretta and Beatrice looked at each other a moment.

"But you don't have a true love," Beatrice said with a puzzled expression.

"Of course I do," I said. "I just don't know yet who he is."

Again they exchanged glances.

"You don't even like anyone very much," Gretta said.

"I like everyone," I said vehemently. "More than I ever have in my life."

I looked down the slope to the village huts nestled like a clutch of gray eggs by the bay.

"Well, yes, but not, perhaps, in a romantic sort of way," Beatrice said.

"We mean you don't love any men," Gretta said in her even, matter-of-fact voice.

"You know very well that I adore all men," I said. "I have always thought them to be the dearest of things."

Beatrice sighed. "In the most general sense—" she began.

"—but not in the specific sense," Gretta finished.

I opened my mouth to contradict them and found that I could not. I grasped their hands. "Well, that must end. I must find a specific man and fall madly in love with him and have him love me back. By tomorrow nightfall. And you must help me."

Beatrice cleared her throat. "Of course we will help you, dear," she said.

"You were indeed stolen by fairies, weren't you?" Gretta said. "And the fairy king will come for you if you do not find your true love."

I sighed. " 'Twas Lord Death I bargained with," I said. Beatrice put her fingertips on her lips. Gretta's hands went limp. How real that made it, saying it thus to my beloved friends.

"Of course," Gretta murmured, as if she suddenly understood everything. She held my eyes with her own. "How else could you have come alive out of the wood?" She turned her gaze toward the forest. "Never have I seen a fairy, but death is as real to me as the scar on my knee. What exactly is the bargain, Keturah?"

"I told him a story and then refused to tell the end. Let me live one day, I said, and I will tell you the end of the story on the morrow. 'Tis a story of love, a love that is greater than death, I told him, and I revealed that I myself would have such a love. He told me that if I could find a love like that before I returned to tell the end of the tale, he would free me of the bond."

I could not bear the hopeless look in Beatrice's eyes, nor the grim one in Gretta's.

Gretta stood tall and put her hands on her hips and looked out over the village. "Now, I wouldn't marry a single one of them," she said. "There's not a perfect one among them. But . . . Tailor comes very close."

"Tailor? Not at all, Gretta. He would be perfect for you," I said.

Gretta looked at me with a shrewd eye, and back to

the bustling village. "When I find a man who will let me increase him in perfections, I will marry," she said. "And Tailor seems not to be a man who will be bossed. He must be perfect for you instead."

"No, Gretta, no. Tailor I could never love. Besides, everyone knows your stitches are the only ones Tailor could bear to look at all his life."

"He has never seen my stitches. He mourns his wife still too greatly to notice such things. No, I have decided, Keturah. I shall never marry. You shall marry Tailor, and I shall be the best spinster and needlewoman in the village, and I shall live to keep my figure and my heart, and I shall grow old and never live to regret unruly children."

"There is Choirmaster," Beatrice said.

"Choirmaster! For Keturah?" Gretta exclaimed. "But I thought *you* liked—" She stopped; then, looking meaningfully at Beatrice, she said, "Ah, yes, Choirmaster—a most eligible bachelor."

"He is intelligent," Beatrice said.

"But gloomy," Gretta replied.

"We could cheer him up," Beatrice said bravely. "He is a devout man."

Gretta answered, "But what about his nostrils?"

"Keturah shall have to try not to look up them."

"But that is impossible!"

"Shush, Gretta," Beatrice said, smiling. "He is an elegant man. And if one can't help but look up his nostrils, at least he keeps his nostrils clean. I've noticed he has a fresh handkerchief every day."

"You know I have always thought well of Ben Marshall," I said slowly.

"Ben Marshall is not bonny enough for you, Keturah," Gretta said.

"You say that about every lad," Beatrice said with a sigh. "Of course he's a handsome lad, Keturah, and well off, too. But there is the tradition—he must marry a Best Cook."

Gretta leaned across the table on her elbows. "He will never love a wife as dearly as he loves his pumpkins and his squashes," she said.

Beatrice said encouragingly, "He is a frugal man, I think."

"Aye, another strike against him," Gretta said, thumping the table and straightening up.

Beatrice frowned at Gretta and then smoothed her frown into forgiveness. Beatrice generously forgave Gretta many times a day.

"Padmoh wants him," Gretta added. "And while she is better suited to him, she is a scold and would make his life a torment."

Padmoh Smith was likely the best cook in the village. She ate eggs every day and sported her girth as proof of it. She had already won Best Cook two years in a row, but Ben Marshall had not yet proposed. Still, Padmoh could make a loaf that would cause a hungry man to weep with desire, and a stew that would make even a fed man beg. Grandmother said that although she was as plain as a fencepost, when a man ate her pie he began to think she was beautiful.

Grandmother also said Beatrice was pretty, though not beautiful, but when she sang, men began to forget that she was not beautiful. Demonstrate talent, said Grandmother often to me, and you will still be loved by a husband when beauty has faded.

But when it had come time for me to demonstrate talent, I did not demonstrate. I could bake a pie and I could tell a story, but neither would win me a husband, Grandmother told me sadly. I might make a fair midwife in time, she said, but it would be my beauty that would get me a husband.

In my mind, any beauty I possessed had not done me good but only caused me grief. Gretta and Beatrice said the other village girls claimed that their sweethearts had been led away by me. That was nonsense. I had no interest in any of their sweethearts, and if the boys spoke to me or stood about me, I was as silent as I could be. I found that I could be very silent. Besides, what need of beauty for a poor peasant girl, living in her own wattle-and-daub with her own peasant husband and her little peasant baby?

I sighed. "A love greater than death," I murmured, and then, just then, I did not know what that meant.

"Well, one thing is certain—we go a-manhunting," Gretta said.

It felt good to have my friends in my confidence, though I confess not my full confidence. I could not bear to tell them what Lord Death had said about the plague.

"I won't let Death have you," said Gretta with great calmness, yet beneath the calmness was a vibrating anger.

I put one hand on her cheek and held Beatrice's hand with my other. "How many die every day under that same heaven which one day cannot be swayed?"

"I will fight him," Beatrice said tearfully—Beatrice, who escorted bugs out of her house with all gentleness. Her pretense of good cheer and bravery had vanished, and I squeezed her hand.

I shook my head. "Beatrice, this is not a man you fight. This is a man before whom you curtsey."

"No," she said. "I hate him."

"Now, now," I said softly. I kissed her hair. Why did it pain me to hear her say this? "It will not be tonight. Go home and rest."

When I went to kiss Gretta, she drew away. "If all else fails, you must fight him, Keturah," she said. "I shall be forever angry with you if you don't."

# III

*I determine to solicit Soor Lily.*

I slept the night away and awoke the next morning with a gasp, having thought myself there with Death in the underland of my dreaming. I looked out my window and saw that the dawn was a gray bird beaked with crimson.

My days lost in the wood had not faded in my memory. I had a remembrance of the hardness of trees and the bitter taste of leaves and the black earth that gave me no water. Plague, I thought. *Plague.*

From my window I could see the forest looming dark and deep, seemingly without end. But I could also see the village, close and safe. No—not safe. My village was in terrible danger, but what could I do to save it?

It began to rain. Our poor and shabby village seemed even poorer and shabbier when it rained. It made the gray houses grayer, and the barns and sheds saggy, as if being wet was more than they could bear. The square turned to mire, the yards to muck. The color went out of the bay, and even the manor looked a great, bare mound of stone.

And yet, I thought, had there ever been so sweet and glorious a place?

"He has allowed his lands to fall to ruin," Lord Death

had said. From that one clue, I hoped, I could perhaps stave off the plague. To save myself I had already devised a plan. I would go to Soor Lily, the village wise woman, and seek a charm by which I might discover my true love. Then, by whatever wiles a decent girl might employ, I would have him wed me this very day.

I had been afraid of Soor Lily all my life, and I was not alone. Her seven enormous sons protected her from those who would drive her away. Still, many of her worst critics in their time of need had gone to her for medicines and potions, and for a price Soor Lily had helped them. Now my fears had been adjusted, too, and I would go to her.

No sooner had I done that than I would go to John Temsland and seek his help against the plague, though by what means I knew not.

The rain stopped and the sun burned away the moisture in the mud and mire. A white haze settled knee deep over the village. Two children ran laughing through it, and the cows dipped their heads in it to graze.

I lay back on my pillow to see the stone hearth, the trestle table, the benches painted with flowers and birds, the thatch ceiling above, hard as oak. In the corner was Grandmother's chest, which stored my old cornstalk doll and linens for my someday wedding. Everything was the same, yet everything was different. Last Sabbath, the cottage in which I had been reared seemed tiresomely small and drafty. Today, it seemed the dearest cottage in Angleland. Bunches of herbs hung from the ceiling: wormwood, feverfew, lungwort, and marjoram. Last Sabbath I barely noticed them; today they were the sweetest scents in God's kingdom. Strange, thought I, that only yesterday I had been about to die, and here I was today for the first time alive.

I thought of my friends Gretta and Beatrice, and remembered wistfully how, as children, we would whisper together as we imagined our true loves. Would mine be someone from the town of Marshall? Or maybe someone who had come a great distance to live in Tide-by-Rood? Even as a young girl, Gretta would say scornfully that no one of any worth would come to our ragged little village. I had agreed heartily, but Beatrice dreamed of a traveling musician who would come to take her away.

Perhaps our true loves would be found among those we knew already—but there we would pause and shake our heads. Gretta would list the qualities she would insist upon in a husband, and Beatrice and I would roll our eyes. "There is no man that perfect, except my father," said Beatrice. "And he is taken."

"And you, Keturah—what of you?" Gretta would ask.

"I? I will marry my own true love, and I care not who he is, how old or young, how poor, how fat or thin," I would reply.

"Ah, Keturah, you are as beautiful as the women who populate your tales," Beatrice would say. "You shall perhaps marry a knight or a duke."

"Only if he is good enough for her," Gretta would say.

"I would marry Hermit Gregor if he was my true love," I would answer stoutly, and we would dissolve into giggles.

Though I was very young, I meant what I said, and it was as true today as it had been then.

Yes, we had all then dreamed of true love. Repenting of traveling musicians—perhaps because none came to Tide-by-Rood—Beatrice had determined to marry a man of God. She would sing in heaven's choir, she vowed, and she embroidered crosses on all her underthings. Gretta, finding fault with the most faultless of men, declared there was no man fit to be her husband. Still, she had always admired Tailor, and in her effort to emulate him she had obtained a certain fame in Tide-by-Rood. In a day she could stitch a cap, in two days a dress. Everyone said a stitch sewn by Gretta did not loosen, and a gown stitched by her felt like heaven's robes. Gretta was not beautiful, but she was perfect in her plainness as she was perfect in everything. Her teeth were perfectly whole and white, her hair curled perfectly around her face, and she had a perfectly trim figure. God had probably feared to make her any other way.

Grandmother awoke, but I stayed still, in my bed, pondering my faceless true love. She added kindling to the banked embers and knelt to pray.

"God, I thank thee for the trial of the lass, and pray for strength to live to see her wed. And if it be not greedy to ask, I pray she be happily wed. Thy will. Further, watch over the old parson, and tell him that Dan Fieldbottom is stealing the holy water to sprinkle his cows. Thy will. And wilt thou thicken the frumenty, that I may lay more by for the winter. Thy will. Amen." I added my own silent amen, and my own prayer for my village, my friends, and my dear grandmother.

If my first breaths were of mourning, it was tempered by the blessing of being weaned on love. Grandfather and Grandmother Reeve raised me with all the tenderness of true parents and all the patience of grandparents. It was not just their kindness to me that I remarked, even at a young age—for I compared my own upbringing with that of others—but also their love for each other.

When Grandfather died, Lord Temsland, who was known for his frugality, gave Grandmother a small pension for the remainder of her days. I would be left alone, without protection, after she died. She wished to see me wed so she could die in peace, she said, knowing that then I would not have to hire myself out a spinster for my share of flour and pork.

We were not starving on Lord Temsland's pension, but neither was there any danger of our ever being fat. Grandfather had died without leaving a dowry for me, but Grandmother expressed great hopes that my beauty might dazzle a man enough to take me as I was.

I had no desire to marry a man who wanted me only for my beauty, if it was true I had it, and so I had not cooperated with my grandmother's aspirations. I covered my hair with a brown scarf, spent little attention on my dress, and refused to learn the subtle feminine arts. My stubbornness served me well. So far no one had declared any love for me. Today, I decided, I would not wear a scarf.

The wheat berries that had been soaking in the pot all night began to simmer over the small fire. Grandmother gave it a quick stir, and came to rouse me. When she bent over my bed to prod me, I clasped her round the neck, drew her to me, and kissed her hard and full upon the cheek.

She smiled at me. "Up, then, Keturah," she said tenderly.

"Yes, Grandmother." I leapt from my bed.

Grandmother milked and I made biscuits, though I was slow with fatigue, and so there was hot bread and butter with our porridge, and warm milk and stewed plums also.

When we had finished, Grandmother reached out and stroked my hair. "Keturah, you must have no more adventures. It is unseemly for a girl of marriageable age. Eat—come, you must have more! Surely you have a high appetite after starving for three days."

But my appetite was satisfied, and I laid down my spoon.

"Grandmother," I asked after a time, "who commands Death? Is anyone greater than he?"

She looked at me, puzzled, and then shook her head. "What thoughts you get, child!"

"Tell me, Grandmother. If we do not speak of him, how will I know how to greet him, or what manner of address I should give him, and what my conversation should be when he comes to me?"

She thought a moment, perhaps thinking of her daughter, her son-in-law, and her husband. "One is greater than death," Grandmother said, "and that is life. For life will be, and work as he may, death must bow in the end to life. When death came for my daughter, life gave me you to comfort my heart. But hear me, child. People don't like to hear death's name. If you are in polite company, he is not spoken of."

"But he has touched every one of us, Grandmother," I said. "Who does not have a loved one that he has not robbed away? We should speak of him. He is to everyone familiar."

"Nevertheless."

I knew that word meant that she would speak no more about it. But I was not ready to end our talk. "Grandmother," I said shyly, "what is love?"

She looked steadily at me, as if trying to determine whether I was being impertinent. My question, however, was sincere, for though I knew what marriage was and how some loves looked and how babies came, still I did not know how love was supposed to feel.

She said, "Do you not love the babies you tend while their mothers are afield?"

"Yes," I said, "but . . ."

"It is all of a one, my dear, all of a one. There's that baby who is loved, and then one day he loves so as to make another baby. Wear our souls out in love, we do, or looking for it."

She leaned closer to me. The color of Grandmother's eyes was hard to tell, the sun had bleached them so, but they were quick and piercing.

"Now I will tell you a true thing, child, and if you are wise you will remember it. The soul, it longs for its mate as much as the body. Sad it is that the body be greedier than the soul. But if you would be happy all your days, as I was with your grandfather, subdue the body and marry the soul. Look for a soul-and-heart love."

A soul-and-heart love, I thought. Yes, that was what I

would have, and I was minded of my urgency to see Soor Lily for a charm.

I asked, "What chores today, Grandmother?"

"Lass, everyone who came to mourn with me did chores enough to last a week. The women cleaned and washed, Ben Marshall cared for the garden, and Tailor did all my mending and tanned a fleece. Tobias did the yard, and Gretta and Beatrice did all the carding and spinning. Take the day for your own, child," Grandmother said, "but go not one step into the forest. I won't lose you again."

That command I wished with all my heart I could obey.

⌁

I had two errands—to speak to John Temsland or his father, and to visit Soor Lily. While the latter was the easier to accomplish, it was the more dreaded.

Soor Lily lived near the road to Marshall, a short way into the green gloom of the forest, with her seven great sons, each the size of two men, who loved her and obeyed her slavishly and would not leave her for a wife. Though the air was still as I entered the wood, leaves of the trees whispered and seemed to bend, as if they were a little more alive than other trees for living near Soor Lily.

When I came to her house, I saw that the door was of oak and enormous, so that her boys, I supposed, might enter in without ducking, as they must do to enter any other house of the village. Not that they were often invited.

As I stood nervously before the door, I saw two of her big boys peering from behind the outhouse, and two more in her huge and mysterious garden. I shouldn't be here, I thought. I should speak to John Temsland first. But even as I turned to go, Soor Lily opened the door.

"Come in, Keturah," she said, half bowing. Her manner was unsurprised, as if she had been expecting me.

"You know my name?" I asked. We had never spoken to each other before.

"Everyone is speaking of you today, and not in quiet voices. But before, I knew you for your beauty." She spoke in a soft, watery voice. " 'Twas no fairies you saw in the wood, Keturah," she said, and I felt glad that she did not believe it.

Soor Lily had been well named. Her walk was measured so that she seemed to float like an autumn lily in a pond. Her clothes she wore in layers like petals, and no one could tell if she was fat or thin. Her skin was pale and waxy, her expression unreadable.

The furniture in her home was of large proportions. Great chairs made of rough-hewn logs and a table almost as big and heavy as Lord Temsland's were set before a gigantic fireplace. Soor Lily's pots, the size of cauldrons, hung from the ceiling, along with nets of bulbs and bunches of drying herbs. A great wooden closet stood against the wall opposite the fireplace, its carved doors discreetly closed. It was all very tidy and clean, and there was no evidence that Soor Lily was a witch.

Though she was.

She sat me in one of the great, solid chairs. In it, my feet did not quite touch the ground, though I was as tall as any woman. I listened for sounds of her big sons, but all was quiet.

She curtseyed a little and then laid out two cups. She wore her hair unbound. "Have some tea. You must be tired from your long walk. So tired. Here is tea. Here, here, my beauty . . . So nice to know there is someone in the parish more vilified than I."

Her voice was a chant, soothing and gentle and throaty.

"I don't believe in love potions," I said stoutly, refusing to touch the tea.

"No, no, you don't," she said quietly, reassuringly. She put warm scones before me, each the size of a pie plate. She hovered around me, at once diffident and attentive, like a bird brooding over her chick, lightly touching my shoulder, my back, my arm. Finally she sat at the table beside me and looked at me as if she were hungry and my eyeballs were just what she had been craving.

"I don't believe in sorcery, and I don't believe in love sorcery most of all," I said, though the defiance in my voice had lost its edge.

"No, not at all," she said. She brushed all the words from the air with her long, spider-leg fingers. "Not at all, my dear, my heart." Her words disappeared into breathy nothingness, as if from moment to moment she forgot what she was saying.

I thought I would stand and leave, now, now, but I did not, for I could hear the wind in the forest around me.

"Is it true?" I whispered at last. "Is it true that you can

make a charm that would show me my true love?"

"Oh yes, it is true," she said with sad resignation. "True love. Mmm—the highest of magics."

"I will have it," I said, sounding braver than I felt.

"You will have it," she said, nodding to herself.

I waited some time, looking at her, but she did not look at me. She studied the fire as if waiting for a phoenix to rise out of the flames.

"Well?" I said at last.

She glanced at me, cleared her throat, and went back to studying the fire.

"Soor Lily, I said I would have it."

She turned glittering eyes upon me, and I could have sworn they had become as hard as amber. "Yes. Yes, you would have it," she said low, almost in a whisper. "But there is the small matter of the price."

Ah, the price. The price was why people feared Soor Lily, for it was not always money she asked for. "I am poor," I said. "You know I am poor."

"Poor, poor," she said sympathetically, but there was no sympathy in her face. She studied the fire again. At last she said, in a voice that was hypnotic in its quiet power, "But there is a price you can pay."

My skin prickled from my scalp to the soles of my feet. "Then name it," I said.

She slowly reached across the table and gripped my hand in hers. It was as strong as a man's. "All the things I could ask of you, Keturah. Couldn't I ask you to let me live forever? Mmm. I could ask to see my departed mother—oh, the questions I would have for her. What was that recipe against the toothache? She told me, of course she did, but I have forgotten. No, Keturah, my beauty, I want none of these things. But come."

She beckoned to me, and I followed her, wooden-legged, to the doorway of another room. There, on a massive bed, lay one of her sons, a boulder of a man. Fevered and distressed, he was not conscious that we were there.

"He is sick," I said.

"So clever you are," said Soor Lily with cloying sweetness. "Yes, he is very sick."

"Why don't you cure him?"

"Precisely," she said. "Exactly. Just so. Why don't I? Is that not what anyone would ask? Who would come to me for cures if they saw I could not cure one of my own sons? But my art, unlike yours, has no power over death." Here she leaned forward very close to me and peered into my face.

I leaned away from her. "How—how did you hear . . . ?"

"Do I not know all things about the forest?" she whispered.

"Then you know I have no power but have only made a bargain."

She shrugged slowly, but I knew she did not believe me.

She shut the door, and silently we went back to the table before the fire. I was so angry and afraid that I could not speak. I thought to leave, but I could not leave empty-handed. I stared at the fire, and Soor Lily stared at me.

At last she said, "You make me broody, you do, for a

girl—a girl of my own. A man-child takes no interest in woman wisdom. Who will learn my recipes as I learned from my mother?"

I glanced at the bulgy bags of roots and things that hung from her ceiling. I could think of no answer. Who would come here, day after day, into the deep, greeny gloom of the wood to learn her dark recipes?

At last I said, half whispering, "Do you know him, too?"

She nodded. "We all know Lord Death. Do I see him as you do? No. But it is closeness to him that imbues my stuffs with power. What is a love potion without the breath of him upon it? How can I make a healing draught without sensing from which direction he comes? One day you will understand, Keturah, that he infuses the very air we breathe with magic."

As she spoke, I thought I saw his face in the fire, his eyes hot as embers, losing all patience with me if I were to ask for the life of her baby giant.

"I have no power over Lord Death," I said weakly. "I see him, but he has no regard for my wishes."

"He will not live the night," Soor Lily said, glancing toward the bedroom where her son lay.

"Nor perhaps shall I," I said. "But—but I will see what I can do."

She nodded. There were tears in her eyes.

"So I will have my charm," I said.

She nodded again. "For you," she said, "my most powerful magic."

She stood up and stared into her kitchen, bracing

herself on the back of the chair. She looked as if she were going to have to commit some foul deed against her will, so white was she, yet resolute.

"First the distillate," she said. She went to her cupboard and removed a small vial with only her thumb and forefinger. Her lip curled in distaste. Carefully she put three drops in a small bowl and stepped away from it. She said, "This will be a pure love, a pure and . . ." She looked at me and stopped speaking.

"It needn't be fancy," I said, glad now that she had begun. "One true love," I said, "preferably one who will give me a little house of my own to clean, and a wee fine baby too."

"Yes, yes," she said, "nothing fancy. It's bad enough without making it fancy. Second, the infusion."

She took a small bottle from beneath a bag of cabbages. She poured the contents into the bowl with the other liquid and swirled it around and around, then gazed into the bowl as if she could see an unpleasant future at the bottom.

"Ahh," she said, almost sadly. "This will be a deep love, deep as . . ." She glanced at me and fell silent.

"Deep?" I said, almost smiling now. "Of course, deep— can you make a charm strong enough to find such a love?"

"I am an artist," she said firmly.

She dug into an opened trunk and rummaged. She took out a half-filled jar.

"Third, the decoction!" she said. Her head shook as if she regretted finding it. She struggled to her feet, grunting, and carefully poured a little in. A thread of smoke floated out of the bowl. "Oh," she murmured. "Oh, lass, 'tis a passionate love you will have."

"Aren't you almost done?" I asked. My courage was beginning to fail me.

"This will be the best love charm I have ever made," she said.

From her apron pocket she drew a small, glistening thing. She plopped it unceremoniously into the bowl.

"What is that?" I asked in horror, though I suspected I knew the answer.

"The charm," she said, "so when you see your true love, you will know him."

"It—it is an *eye*," I said.

"Yes," she said. "Put it in your apron pocket. Touch it and you will feel it looking. When it grows completely still, you will have found your true love. And let me assure you, Keturah, that there is one for you. I felt it powerfully."

I could not tell if it was gratitude or pity or the fumes of the potion on her fingers that made me love her at that moment. "Thank you, Soor Lily."

She folded a small cloth around the eyeball and tied it with a lace ribbon. "From my wedding veil," she said, pointing to the lace. I reached for the charm, but she pulled it back. "Tonight—you must ask him tonight."

I nodded. "You can be sure I will see him tonight," I said.

She handed it to me at last, and I took it from her and left as quickly as I could, somewhat relieved but dreading the price.

And now, having secured a way to find my true love, I determined to speak to John Temsland.

# IV

*What happens when I test the charm's power;*
*I ask Cook for a lemon; an unexpected visitor;*
*John Temsland says, "We are doomed."*

As I walked in the village I gripped the charm and looked deep into the eyes of every man I met upon the road, just in case.

If any of them was my true love, I did not recognize him, nor did the eye. It flickered and shook in my hand like a trapped beetle. Most of the men would not look at me for long, fearful of one who had likely communed with fairies.

I picked my way around muddy ruts in what passed for the road into Tide-by-Rood, and stopped at the outskirts to consider my village.

Across the bay, the forest marched right to the banks, as if it would cross and wring our village away with its vast roots. Behind the village we kept the forest at a distance only by ax and saw. Nearest the water was the church with its blackened bell, then the half-fallen smithy and the infested mill, and then the cottages going up the hill, planted like wilting flowers in a tiered garden. At the top, where the rise leveled off and the forest began, was the manor, Lord Temsland's great house. Once it had been grand, but now the roof needed repairing and the whole of it looked neglected. West of the manor was the apple orchard, and just beyond that, also at the edge of the forest, stood our worn little cottage, with nothing but the garden between us and the deep, wild wood.

Still, the sun shone with familiar cheer.

I could not imagine the plague on this sunny day. Hadn't I heard how whole villages perished in a fortnight? How little ones wept in their own filth, wondering why their parents did not come to comfort or feed, not understanding that they were dead? How neighbors boarded up the homes of the stricken while those inside died of the plague or, worse, of starvation? How friend ran away from friend, lover from lover, mother from child?

Surely not, I thought, shaking my head in disbelief and horror. Surely not Tide-by-Rood! And if so, what words could I use to persuade John Temsland to do something? I continued on my way, letting my scarf fall back a little and looking boldly about as I walked. I gazed at every man and squeezed the charm, but still the charm searched and searched.

I headed toward the manor, but it seemed I was not the only one. The entire village, almost, was gathering at the manor. Gretta and Beatrice caught up with me and linked arms.

"Are you coming to cheer on the men, Keturah?" Beatrice asked, flushed and panting for breath.

"No, I am going to see John Temsland. I must speak with him."

"John Temsland? But he will not be seeing anyone," Gretta said.

"Today is the hunt—the hunt of the hart who lured you into the forest," Beatrice said.

"But I would not have him hunted!" I exclaimed, remembering his royal beauty.

"You could not stop them," Gretta said.

"But I must try." Now my errand was doubled—not only must I tell John Temsland what Lord Death had revealed to me, but I must beg him, or his father, to call off the hunt. As I looked for the young lord, I also clutched the charm and plunged among the gathered men, seizing the opportunity to see which of them was my true love. The eye darted, flickering back and forth in my hand until I myself was jittery and the flesh of my arm crawled. The eye settled on no one.

I looked at old and young, fair and plain, tall and small. I gazed at fat and thin, hairy and bald, rich and poor. Almost all the men of the village were there, though only those rich enough to own a horse would venture into the wood for the hunt. The rest cheered them on, made bets as to whose arrow would bring the stag down, and told my stories of the stag and how he had eluded hunters in the past. Seeing them so animated made me feel the importance of my original errand more acutely.

Suddenly I saw Lord Temsland, though not his son, and I pushed through the crowd toward him. "My lord!" I called. "Please, my lord!"

But before I could reach him, Lady Temsland came on a horse and spoke urgently to him.

"A messenger!" I heard Lord Temsland exclaim. "But we've never had a messenger from the king, nor any visitor at all."

"Husband," she said, "the hunt must wait. The king has sent his most trusted servant, Duke Morland, and I have persuaded him to take his midday meal with us. Come." Without waiting, she spun her horse around, and Lord Temsland followed her.

"Set traps for the hart!" Lord Temsland called as he rode away. Some men entered the wood to perform the task, but I sighed with relief as most of the men began to stream away toward the village, distracted from the hunt by a desire to see a messenger from the king. Somehow, in the press of people, I had missed John.

I turned back to the wood, thinking that the young lord might yet be there, but instead Ben Marshall stood before me, tall and comely. "Keturah," he said, "you are still pale. You have not fully recovered."

"I slept well," I replied, and then realized the eye had stopped. No, not stopped, but slowed. It was rolling up and down in my hand as if it were taking Ben in, considering him from the top of his head down to his sod-stained boots.

I felt myself blushing, as if it were I myself who was looking him up and down.

"My, it is warm," I said, though it was not. *Stop*, I told the eye in my mind. *Stop*. But it did not stop. It continued to slide in my hand, rolling up and down and side to side, as if it were trying to see around him, as if my true love might be standing behind Ben. It was all I could do not to squeeze the eye into stillness.

"Are you planning what you will make for the cooking contest at the fair, Keturah?" he asked. He said it flirtatiously, as if those were courting words.

"Oh, yes. Of course," I said, and blushed again for my lie. Slow was good, I thought, thinking of the eye. Or at least hopeful. The eye needed only time, though time was, alas, in short supply.

"Come to the manor with me, and let us see the messenger from the king," Ben said.

We walked, and he talked of everyday things, and speculated upon the marvel of a visit from the king's messenger. I wondered at how mundane his concerns would seem to him if only he knew what I knew.

Through it all, the eye kept rolling. Perhaps it was not working properly, and would not until Soor Lily's price was paid. Or would it not stop for Ben because one had to be Best Cook to marry him? I scarcely heard a word Ben said after that, so busy was I with thoughts of finding a foolproof way to win Best Cook. If only I had more time!

I looked up at the sky to see how much more day I had.

How had the sun, which moved so slowly when I was doing chores or waiting for the common fire, become a swooping bird of prey? I shadowed my eyes with my hand to look at it, my enemy, and in that moment I knew how to secure the prize of Best Cook for myself.

Ben was saying something about Farmer Dan and holy water, but I interrupted him.

"I must go!" I said. "Goodbye!" And I gathered my skirts to run.

"Keturah . . . ," he called after me.

"I have a plan," I called back, "to win me Best Cook!"

Along the way, Gretta and Beatrice intercepted me. "Do you go to find John Temsland, Keturah?" Beatrice asked as they matched their strides to mine.

"First I must go to Lord Temsland's kitchen," I said.

"His kitchen?" Gretta exclaimed.

"But why are you going to the kitchen, Keturah?" Beatrice asked.

"To obtain a lemon."

Both Beatrice and Gretta stopped. "A lemon?" they asked at the same time.

"A lemon," I said, continuing briskly. "'Tis a fruit, dears. Grandfather spoke of it once, after he went to the king's court with Lord Temsland."

"A lemon!"

"They say it is as yellow as the sun," I said.

"We know that," Gretta said, "but . . ."

"And more sour than a crabapple." My plan was becoming clearer to me as I spoke. "Yet with it I could make a dish that would cause Ben Marshall to forget all other dishes, a dish that would cause him to forget all other foods and all other women. It will make me the Best Cook of the fair, and he will ask me to marry him, and I will say yes." I looked at my friends and smiled. "'Tis said the queen has lemon in her tea at Easter and Christmas. I am hoping Cook has one."

"So your true love is—Ben Marshall?" Beatrice ventured.

"Yes," I said, "or at least the charm gives me hope that it is so. I shall do all in my power to love him. With all my heart. Undyingly."

"Then we shall come with you," Gretta said.

Once at the manor kitchen, I knocked, and old Cook came to the door. "Who is it, then?" she asked, peering at me. She was so farsighted she could not tell a face. She could smell, though. "Must be the Reeve girl. Much gossip about you today. You still smell like the forest. And Beatrice and Gretta are never far behind. Thank heavens you've all come."

"Cook, we cannot stay."

"You must stay." As she spoke she herded us into the kitchen. "I have the aches today, and it is today of all days the lord receives a messenger of the king. Dinner must be ready, and it must be fine."

"But Cook," I said, "I came only to fetch a lemon."

Cook stopped. "A what?"

"A lemon, Cook, so that she can win Best Cook at the fair," said Beatrice. "So that Ben Marshall will marry her, so that—" Gretta nudged Beatrice, and she fell silent.

Cook laughed. Her teeth were all brown but strong. "A lemon!" she said to me. "Is that all, child? Well, let me check the larders for a stray one. But they are very dear. If I give you a lemon, first you must cook. You and your friends."

She dragged me along, grinning ferociously, as if she were twice my size and not half of it. "You will do pastries today. I know you can do pastries. And watch the pig, too."

As Cook led me into the bowels of her kitchen, I thought that this was how Jonah must have felt in the belly of the great fish. It was dark and hot, and slimy with blood and guts and grease. Smoke and fire filled the room, and the smell of rot and garbage overcame the smell of roasting. Someone shouted and someone else moaned.

Cook set me to my task, and I worked pastry and turned the spit until my back was a rigid board of pain. In the flames of the fire I thought I saw Death's fine face, and sometimes I thought I heard his laughter. Cook set tasks for Gretta and Beatrice as well. I told myself the pastry was not a bad price for a lemon, the prize that would foil Death's plan.

After what seemed hours, I grabbed Cook as she scuttled by me. "Cook, surely by now I have earned my lemon," I said.

"No, not yet," she said. "Keep going."

"How do I know you even have a lemon?" I asked, knowing she was a sly old thing.

"Oh, I do, I do."

"Let's see it, then," I said.

"Oh, I don't show my precious lemons to just any village girl," she said.

So I made pies until I had repented of every sin I had ever committed, including coming for a lemon before I had asked John to do something to stay the plague. I confessed every sin out loud to the roasting pig. Whenever the pastor spoke of death, in the same breath he spoke of hell and fire. If death was anything like Lord Temsland's kitchen, I had no desire to go there. I wondered if Lord Death ruled the good or the bad, and while I could remember no evil in the darkness of his eyes, I could tell they had seen much suffering. But then, it mattered not whether he was lord of the happy dead or the sad; I wanted no part of either.

At last Cook came and declared the pastries fine and the pig perfectly done, and I collapsed onto a stool.

"Now gravy," she said, putting a buttery finger under my chin.

"No," I said resolutely. "I know nothing about gravy."

"Can you not cook, then?" she asked. "Shall I tell this to Ben Marshall?"

"Please, no! I can do pies. Meat pies and fruit pies. Pies. Only pies, but I am better at pies than Padmoh."

She studied me, realizing perhaps that she had met a soul as stubborn as her own. "Come," she said. "With the face of an angel you will serve, then. You can walk and carry a tray, can you not?"

I stood. "Yes. But before I take another step, I shall have my lemon."

"Nay, but only serve, lass, and I shall find you my greenest lemon."

"Green! But lemons are yellow."

"That is what I meant—yellow."

"You don't have one!" I exclaimed. I grabbed her by the nose. "Confess, old brown tooth, you don't have any lemons."

"No, I don't, foolish girl," she said, smacking my hand. "There is not a one to be had in these parts, though I've heard one can be bought for its weight in gold in the Great Market. But if you love Lord Temsland and do not wish to disgrace him before the king's messenger, then you shall serve!"

"Then I will ask the lord myself for a lemon," I said stubbornly to Cook.

"Ask," she said cheerfully. "And while you are at it, ask for half his holdings, an equally small thing."

Gretta, Beatrice, and I were given heavy trays of trenchers to carry into the great hall. We were mournful at first, but when we saw the crowd, and saw that we would have a server's close view of the messenger, Duke Morland, our hearts were cheered. The duke was dressed in turquoise silk, a man very different from Lord Temsland, who dressed in woolens and furs and had little time for much else but the hunt. Beatrice blushed when she served the messenger, and whispered to me that he smelled like a begonia.

The duke surveyed the feast before him, then smiled as one would who was served mudcakes by a little child. He concentrated on his food, chewing thoroughly, as if the meat were tough. Young John Temsland picked at his meat and ate nothing. Lady Temsland, too, ate lightly. Only Lord Temsland seemed to enjoy his food, licking his fingers and sopping up the sauce with Cook's good bread, as if he were alone in the room, relaxed and unconcerned.

Lady Temsland and the duke exchanged pleasantries. As I served, I tried to attend more to the needs of John. I had not forgotten my gratitude that he had found me at the wood's edge and carried me home, nor that he had promised me an interview.

"Keturah," he said, smiling, when he saw that it was I who served him at table. "Are you well?"

"Well enough, sir," I said, and returned his smile.

The messenger noted John's kind words to me, a peasant, and frowned in obvious disapproval. John flushed at this and then said, with seeming care that Duke Morland hear him, "You are far too lovely to serve, Keturah Reeve, and too recently recovered from your adventure. Please, take off your apron and sit at table with us."

"Oh no, sir, I . . ."

"It is my express desire," he said, and I knew by his tone that I would anger him if I did not obey.

Numbly, I sat down at the table, but I did not remove my apron with its precious charm. Many villagers had gathered in the corners and shadows of the common room to see a messenger of the king. I could feel their eyes full upon me now, though I stared at the table and would not look up. Of all the eyes, it was those of the messenger's, full of disdain, that I felt most.

Lord Temsland also seemed somewhat surprised, but he said nothing. The gracious Lady Temsland behaved as if everything was as it should be.

Gretta served me once, saying "Ma'am" with a little smile.

I stole glances at John. He had always been mischievous, but brave of heart. Though he was bucked off several times as a lad, he'd never learned to fear a horse and had become a masterful rider. Once he'd climbed a great tree and couldn't get down. He had to be rescued by Cass

Porter, and his father made him chop Cass's wood for a month as punishment. John had done it in good humor, and had even chopped the wood another fortnight—as his own apology, he had said.

I confess that I ate little, instead holding the eye while I looked at the men in the crowd. Soon, though, I could not bear its quivering, and I took my hand away.

It was not until the pastries were all passed that Duke Morland stated the king's business.

"The fame of your land reaches the king," the man said in a voice loud enough to be heard throughout the hall.

The room fell silent. Tide-by-Rood, famous?

"I am honored, sir," Lord Temsland answered in his deep, gruff voice. John, his mouth half-full of food, glanced uncomfortably at his mother.

The duke dabbed at his mouth, laid his napkin down primly, and leaned toward Lord Temsland. His voice was haughty. "The king has heard of the, ahem, great things you have supposedly done with this corner of the kingdom which he so generously gave you. He has heard"—here the messenger cast a dubious eye around the room—"that you have the best corner of all."

Lord Temsland smiled broadly, stretched back in his chair, and put his arm on the back of his son's chair. "Indeed I do," he said. "The king was generous. There is no hunting anywhere as fine as in my forest lands."

Everyone in the village knew how Lord Temsland had come to be lord of these lands. Many years before, the king had invited him to a hunt in the royal woodlands. The king did well that day, felling a six-point buck. All praised him until Lord Temsland, returning last, was discovered to have landed an even bigger buck. Soon thereafter some lords who were jealous of Lord Temsland used the moment of the king's displeasure to persuade him that Lord Temsland should be humbled. His great lands near the court were taken away, and he was given a tiny manor in the southwest corner of the kingdom with only two villages, Tide-by-Rood and Marshall. "I have thought that with a good lord to oversee these lands, much could be done with them," the king told him. "But at least it is rich in forest lands and teeming with game. With your hunting abilities, you'll surely be happy there."

Indeed, once he got over his resentment at being virtually banished from the court and from titled society, Lord Temsland was happy enough here, and his wife and son loved their lands and people. But it was well known that Lord Temsland was the poorest of the lords, and whenever he went to court, many mocked him for his misfortune. Since neither the king nor the lords ever ventured this far, Lord Temsland had taken to making up stories about his lands—how the villagers were as fair and good as the people of Great Town.

"In particular, the king has heard that you have a fine fair each year," the messenger said.

"That, sir, is true," John Temsland said. John seemed glad that something the duke had said was true.

"I am sent to announce that the king will come to Tide-by-Rood at fair time," the duke said, "with an entourage of his greatest lords. He wishes to see your lands and your village and witness for himself how . . . *fine* they are." He cleared his throat. "Since he comes at fair time, I am instructed to say that His Majesty offers a prize—his shoe full of gold and a wish granted—to the one who most delights him at the fair."

The entire hall rang with silence for a moment. Lord Temsland flushed and ran a hand over his whiskers. At last Lady Temsland said in her soft, gentle voice, "Please tell the king we are deeply honored, and we look forward to his visit."

Duke Morland nodded once, and stood. "Now, if you will grant me leave." He did not wait for permission. His eye took in the shabby manor, the shoddily dressed servants, and he positively smirked as he strode out.

There was a hush among the noble family and the servants alike. All at once everyone began to speak: "The king is coming to Tide-by Rood! The king is coming to our fair!" But I heard Lady Temsland say to her husband, "You have been boasting, my dear."

John Temsland beside me said, "We are doomed."

# V

*Showing how I lost my fear of nearly everything;
what passes in the woods between me and a mysterious
poacher, which chapter must be hidden from
the eyes of blushing young maidens.*

"Sir," I said quietly, my voice completely lost in the hubbub.

"John," said John glumly to the table.

"John, sir, forgive me if I remind you that you were so gracious as to grant me an interview."

"Of course," he said distractedly. "I have not forgotten. I will send Henry for you. Soon."

"It is of the greatest importance. It has to do with the safety of the village."

"That sounds very important indeed," he said. But I could plainly see that he felt that nothing could be as important as what the messenger had just announced.

"Why shouldn't I boast?" Lord Temsland said loudly to his wife and the audience. "Is this not the best parish in the king's dominion?"

We glanced furtively at one another's unmended clothes, and at our shoes and stockings, stained and muddied by our untended pathways. We cast our minds with shame upon our unpainted doors and shutters that hung crookedly, and upon the refuse piles in our yards that had been allowed to grow too large. Even the manor walls wanted chinking. The straw on the manor floor was clean—Lady Temsland saw to that—but somewhere the roof leaked and dripped into our silence. Just then a cow that had escaped an unrepaired corral shoved her head into the doorway and lowed.

Gradually everyone's excitement died away. I felt sad for them, and for me. There had been so much life in everyone's enthusiasm for the king's visit. People were still gathering into the hall, but as they came, their smiles faded to see the somber faces of their fellows.

Suddenly I had an idea—one that could well humble Death's proud look and accomplish my desire. The king's visit was surely willed of God, I thought, and I gathered the courage to express my idea.

"If you please, lord, this *is* the best parish in Angleland," I said. "But for small things, who could be richer than we? We all have full bellies, and warm fires to sit by, and Choirmaster's beautiful music of an evening. We have many old men and women, and our lord judges us fairly . . ."

"Sit down!" someone called. "Who are you to speak so?" called another. "She has cast fairy dust on young John," someone else said.

But Lord Temsland seemed pleased by my words. "Let her speak," he said, and the crowd fell into a sullen silence. "It is the Reeve girl, is it not? Speak."

"We are a happy people, just as happy as those in Great Town," I said, trying to sound brave, though my knees shook. "But will the king and the great lords see what we see? We must prepare for the king. We must rid the mill of rats, and build a road, and pave the square—"

"That would cost dear," Lord Temsland interrupted, with a finality that made me take my seat.

But John took up my argument. "Father, it is a fine idea. For this you should open your coffers."

"That gold, my son, is to buy you better lands than these that have been my exile," Lord Temsland said.

A hush fell over the crowd, and John flushed at the words of his father, spoken so publicly.

"You think of your lands as exile, Father. But I was born here. These lands are my home and my inheritance. Let us open the coffers to prepare for the king. We could indeed build a road and pave the square—and improve the church, and repair the cottages! Why should the king's favorites come to gloat?"

Lord Temsland's face exuded pride in his son's words, but he was a stubborn man. "I have a better plan. I will go to the king and make my excuses. I will ask him to delay his visit indefinitely."

"To ask the king to delay his visit will only assure that he will come," Lady Temsland said mildly.

"Nevertheless, I go," said Lord Temsland. He arose and gestured to several of his men. "I will tell him—tell him there is plague or something."

Lord Temsland roared as he strode out, "Roberts, get the horses ready. Webster, make haste to pack what is necessary for the journey." Servants ran to help, and the villagers scattered before him. He did not look back or bid his son or wife adieu.

After he left the hall, the villagers began to chatter like field gulls after the harvest. Lady Temsland stood and raised her hand for silence. She said nothing and seemed to be listening, so we all listened as well. At last we heard the horses of Lord Temsland and his men as they sped away to the king's court.

Lady Temsland now lowered her hand—it trembled a little—and took a ring of keys from her waist. Removing one, she said, "Son, an ancient law tells us that when the lord of the manor is away from his lands, his heir becomes steward of key and coffer. This key, you may find, opens the chests of coin your father has been saving to purchase better lands for you."

John took the key in his hand and smiled at his mother. "The coin will purchase better lands indeed, Mother," he said. "Though not perhaps as my father imagined."

He turned and smiled at me then.

"Sir, we could make this year's fair the best we have ever had—the best in the kingdom," I said.

"Cheeky bold, ain't she?" someone said.

"The young lord don't seem to mind," said another. "P'raps she's tranced him with her stories."

"It will be a celebration in honor of the king," John said to those gathered. "He loves fine clothes and a good hunt and delicious food. We will satisfy his every delight."

The crowd loved their young lord. "Aye, John," they called. Two or three cheered.

"Where is Choirmaster?" John Temsland asked. "Summon him. The king loves music—we will give him music. It will be godly music, and perhaps God will help us."

This time more in the crowd cheered. Already servants were running down the hill to the village to get Choirmaster.

Lord Temsland was afraid of no one, but he revered two offices, that of the king and that of the churchman. The manor was bigger than the parish church, but over the years Lord Temsland had lavished his church with a stained-glass window, a bell that rang for Sabbath and for weddings and funerals, and—glory of glories—an organ.

For three years it sat in the church, a symbol of civilization in Tide-by-Rood, polished to a shine, stately and . . . silent. No one knew how to play it. And then Choirmaster came to our town—a strange thing, for no one came to our town—and brought the organ to life.

Now Lady Temsland, always calm and unruffled, had a slight blush upon her cheek, and said, "Son, we must find some new and wonderful dishes to delight the palate of the king when he comes."

"Send for Cook!" John cried.

Cook came quickly, as if she had been awaiting his summons.

"Here I am, m'lord," she said.

"Undoubtedly you have heard," John said respectfully, for he loved the old woman. When he was an infant, she had nursed him. After he was weaned, she took a place as pie mistress of the kitchen and often made him cinnamon sticks from leftover crust. "The king is coming to our fair," said John. "Be prepared to serve all of your best meats and breads and pies. Perhaps you might also concoct a new dish, Cook, something the king has never had before."

Cook rubbed her soft whiskers. "And what would that be, Johnny?" she asked.

"I don't know. You are the cook."

"Don't forget, young sire, we're just a poor village in the farthest corner of Angleland. Do you think I have anything here to interest a king?"

"You will try, Cook," John commanded, though he was unused to asserting his authority.

"Can't do it," she said bluntly.

I saw Beatrice gasp and Gretta's eyes open wide.

John reddened. Everyone in the room looked from him to Cook and back again. Cook stood her ground.

"You will do as I say," John said firmly.

"Can't, Johnny," she said.

He sputtered, "Cook, you mustn't call me . . ."

"I changed your nappies, sire," she said.

"By the . . . !"

Lady Temsland leaned over and laid a soft hand on her son's. "Perhaps, Cook, you will call him Johnny only when he comes to the kitchen to steal cookies," she said with a small smile. "Dear Cook, I am sure you can come up with something wonderful."

"I am old, lady," Cook said, more humbly.

"Your sons, though?"

"They have learned to cook by rote, lady. Not one has

the gift. They are all three hopeless knaves, taking after their father, who thankfully died years ago."

Lady Temsland nodded understandingly, though she could not entirely quit the smile from her face. "Well then, we shall have to depend upon God for help."

I spoke up. "If I may, lady."

Even Lady Temsland, who was always composed, seemed surprised that I would speak up again. Beatrice blushed for shame in my behalf.

"This Keturah Reeve," Cook said, her whiskers bristling, "she cannot cook."

"Padmoh will help—she won Best Cook. And I can help. We can all help."

Every eye was upon me, but it was John Temsland's eyes that I felt. "And what can you do?" he asked me.

"I can do tricky things with eggs and herbs and cheeses."

"Peasant food," he said, sighing.

"But delicious," I said.

Everyone was shocked that I had contradicted the young lord. My boldness came, perhaps, from remembering that one whom even the young lord must obey wanted to marry me.

"Sir, it is said the queen has a lemon drink every year at Christmas," I said. "Lemon is a precious fruit, but if your lordship could lay hands upon two or three, I could make a dish with them that the queen would love." And one, I thought, that would win me Best Cook at the fair and Ben Marshall for a husband and perhaps even a shoe full of gold.

"Tobias!" John called.

"Sire," said the boy, stepping forward.

"Tobias, might I count on you to search out lemons for Keturah to make a dish for the queen?"

"Yes, m'lord, for her and for you—and the queen, of course."

"Very well. Here—this should be enough." John took a purse of coins from his own vest. "Take a horse. Any one that you choose. And hurry back—we'll need every man's help."

"Yes, m'lord!" Tobias flashed me a smile before he ran toward the stable. In the moment that I watched him go, John Temsland and his mother turned to enter their private apartments, and I had lost my chance for an interview with John.

Still, there were plans in place to clean up the village, and the day was not over.

The villagers began to scatter, planning how they also might win a shoe full of gold and a wish granted. Some returned to their cottages to cook and sew and clean. Tobias hitched up one of the lord's horses. Some of the men were already pacing out the town square to cobble it.

Come, Lord Death, I thought grimly. You shall not have Tide-by-Rood, or me, after all.

My two friends and I linked arms as we walked together from the square. Beatrice spoke eagerly about the upcoming visit of the king, wondering what he looked like and if he had small or large feet, until Gretta hushed her.

"Forgive us our gaiety, Keturah," Gretta said. "We have not forgotten your bargain. In fact, I have devised a plan so you can marry the least imperfect man in the village. I will sew a lady's gown for the queen and say you did it, and it will be so beautiful that you will win the king's shoe, and you will use it for a dowry to wed Tailor."

I smiled gratefully and said firmly. "Thank you, Gretta. But he is for you."

"Nonsense. How can I possibly marry a man whose favorite color is orange?"

"Well, if not he, then Choirmaster," said Beatrice. "But I don't know how to win his heart for you."

As if by saying his name she had conjured him, Choirmaster appeared before us. He had a bag dangling from a stick that he carried over his shoulder, and he was walking toward the forest.

"Choirmaster!" Beatrice called.

He stopped but did not turn around. Then he continued to walk.

"Choirmaster!" she cried, louder this time, and ran with all speed to him. Gretta and I followed more slowly.

Finally he turned about and nodded his head gravely. "Well met, Beatrice," he said. He nodded to Gretta and me.

"Where are you going, Choirmaster?" Beatrice asked.

"Into the forest," he said sadly.

I laid my hand on his forearm. "Good sir, that way is death."

"That I well know, Sister Reeve," he said, and he made to turn himself about and enter the trees. The trees seemed to reach their branches toward him, whispering to him to come, come.

"Sir, what can be so bad?" Beatrice asked with alarm.

"I tried to explain to the young lord," he said. "But he would not listen. The king loves music, he said. You must have the choir sing, he said, well enough to charm a king. Alas, I cannot make a silk purse from a sow's ear. I told him my lead soprano has grown whiskers and become a tenor all of a night, but he would not listen to me. He expects beautiful music. Beautiful! Here in Tide-by-Rood! I would lose my post at best—and perhaps a body part as well, depending on how badly the choir sang. Ah, how did I end up here?"

I knew how Choirmaster had ended up here—people in the richer towns could not bear to be quite as sad and somber as Choirmaster could make them.

"Oh!" Beatrice suddenly cried aloud. "Dear Choirmaster," she said, "I believe I may have a solution to your woes. I mean—I mean, I believe *Keturah* may have a solution to your woes."

"Indeed?" He took out a great white handkerchief and dabbed his stupendous nose with it.

"She—she has a—a cousin, whose name is Bill. And he sings."

"Bill? Why have I never heard of him?"

I wondered the same myself, and then I realized what Beatrice was suggesting. As a girl she could not sing in the choir, but as a boy she could.

"He—he rarely sings, sir, for his mother fears making

the angels jealous," I said with an encouraging look from Beatrice.

"Truly?"

"She will send him to you, and you shall have your soprano, and beautiful music," Beatrice said.

He smiled at her and then me. "Thank you, Keturah." He frowned. "But if he can't sing . . ."

"He can sing the river still, Choirmaster," I said, and Beatrice blushed pink as a spring rose.

"Tell him to come first thing after chores tomorrow."

"And if he comes, Choirmaster," Beatrice said, "will you play a happy song? And will you come to dinner at Keturah's house?"

"If he can sing as you say, anything might be possible," Choirmaster said. He looked at the burden on his shoulder as if he could not remember where he had been going.

We bade him good day, and he turned back toward the church.

"And how, my pretty Beatrice, how will you possibly become a boy by tomorrow morning?" I asked.

"I shall pray," she said, "and as a boy, I shall sing until Choirmaster makes happy music, and then you shall love him and he will marry you in gratitude for the choir, and the king shall give you his shoe full of gold and the wish of your heart."

I did not let her see my smile. I had devised many plans that day, and now I had one more, one that included the happiness of my friends. Though evening was gathering over the forest, my heart was full of hope as we continued home. Lord Death would not have Choirmaster either.

Gretta and Beatrice parted to go to their own homes and talk with their families about the exciting turn of events for Tide-by-Rood, but only after a promise that I would call for them if I had need of anything.

My heart was lighter than my step as I walked the upward path to home, for I felt a strange fatigue in my bones. A breeze out of the forest, cold and scented with bitter pine, reminded me that although work had begun on the village, John Temsland was yet unaware of the grim reason for my plan. And the day was wearing on.

Again I wondered why the eye would roll and roll in the presence of Ben Marshall, and again I suspected that the charm would not tell me once and for true until I had paid Soor Lily's price.

Though the very scent of the forest breeze made my arms gooseflesh, I knew I would pay the price—not only for the charm, but for the honor of it. I could not bear to see even Soor Lily's great lump of a baby son go to Lord Death.

By the time I arrived at home, Grandmother was at work with the evening meal and solicited my help as soon as I crossed the threshold.

"Into the garden with you, and fetch me beets and peas, dear."

I went, and wearily I gathered. I did not look at the forest. I picked the peas closest to the cottage, and thought the whole time how I might help Beatrice become a boy and where I might procure boys' clothing. I had almost enough beets and peas for the meal when I heard thrashing in the forest just beyond the garden.

I was so afraid, I dropped the vegetable basket. Perhaps it was Lord Death building me a marriage house, I thought. Angrily I put the vegetables back in the basket, and then listened again. More thrashing, and so I cautiously approached the forest's edge and peered into the green gloom.

Now I could hear that the thrashing had the wild sound of an animal. I sighed with relief. Then, above that, was a human sound.

I stepped carefully into the wood, assuring myself with each step that it would be the last, that I would go no closer. Just when I was about to turn back, I came upon a clearing, and in it, a sleek doe, and beside her, a young man in brown wool and green. His head was deeply hooded, and from within his hood he was speaking to the doe. He had not seen me. He had one hand stretched out to the doe, as if to calm her, and in the other he held a knife. I did not know his voice for certain, but it was familiar.

I crept closer.

I could see now that the doe had walked into a snare. Her hind leg was pulled taut and trembling by a rope. Quietly, so I would not startle her, but loud enough for the youth to hear, I said, "The lord of our parish will hang you."

He half turned toward me and seemed to consider me from within the shadow of his hood. Very slowly he lifted a single finger before his face.

"Do not silence me, stranger," I said in a voice at once still and stern. "This forest belongs to Lord Temsland, and if you are caught trapping his deer, by the king's law you can be hanged."

"This is not my snare," the youth said quietly. "I only wish to free her."

Speaking with low, gentle words to the doe, the youth approached her. She had thrashed against the rope so hard that her leg was bleeding.

"Why do you wish to free her when you could eat her instead?"

The youth said nothing for a moment, and then nodded toward the deep of the forest. "Because she is his mate," he said.

I looked, and there stood the great hart, still and staring, the beast that had eluded the lord's traps and hunting parties for years, the one I had followed into the forest to meet Lord Death. He seemed to meet my eyes, and for a moment I could not breathe.

In one motion, the youth dived to the stake that held the rope and cut it through with his knife. The doe leapt twenty paces in a bound and was away, the rope still knotted around her foot.

The hart in the shadows cast his round eye upon me and upon the youth for another moment, and then slowly walked after the doe.

The youth stood breathing deeply and put away his knife. I saw that it was a fine knife, but I did not recognize his hands or his stance. He was relaxed now, obviously pleased with himself. He bowed to the retreating back of the hart. "She will worry the knot off," he said, more to himself than to me.

"That is the leader of the herd that razed three haystacks this past winter," I said.

"The very one," said the youth.

"Lord Temsland has been hunting him for a long time and would have hunted him today if it were not for a visit from the king's messenger." An idea had come to me—an answer to Beatrice's prayer. "Did you consider that he may have trapped the doe as bait?"

The young man tipped his head.

"If Lord Temsland knew what you have done," I continued, "you would be hanged by your thumbs for sure. You must do something for me so that I don't tell."

I could see enough of the shadows of his face now to guess that he might be smiling, but I could not be sure.

"At your service, lady," he said. He bowed so low that it might have been mockery.

"I need your clothes," I said.

He said nothing, but neither did he run away.

"Sir, you will obey if you hold your thumbs dear," I said. "I need a set of boys' clothing. Go behind that bush and disrobe."

For a moment he did not move, and then he bowed slightly. He did not go behind the bush. He removed his boots, then his trousers, replaced his boots, and tossed the trousers at my feet. His face was toward me the whole time, as if he were daring me to watch.

I felt myself flush as I picked up the trousers. "The tunic too," I said.

In a single motion he removed his hood and tunic. And

there stood the young lord John Temsland.

I could not help myself. I gasped. Again he bowed.

"I beg your pardon, sir," I choked out, so frozen with fear that I could not release my grip on his clothes.

"There need be no begging, Mistress Reeve," he said, and he smiled gaily.

"But about your thumbs . . ."

"If my father discovered my secret, that for some time now I have been foiling his efforts to have the hart, I would lose my thumbs indeed, son or no," he said. "But it is cold, and I would have my clothes back."

I looked down at his clothes, still in my hands, and remembered that in this very wood I had met Lord Death.

I curtseyed. "I am sorry, sir," I said in a choked voice, "but I need them now. But if you would have them back, I will bring them to the interview you promised me."

I ran, and the evening wind could not cool my flaming face.

I hid the clothes beneath Grandmother's raspberry canes, and hurried into the house with the vegetables for supper. If Grandmother noted my preoccupation and my alarm at every unexpected sound, she was silent on the matter.

# VI

⚜

*A second meeting, and my attempts to delay.*

I ate only a little supper, watching anxiously through the window as the shadows of the forest reached toward the cottage. No, I would not go—I could not go. Not yet, at least. There was still a little time, and Grandmother wished me to come with her to the common fire.

From down in the church the saddest tunes rose and fell like clouds of spring butterflies as we made our way. Most were already at the fire, but if we passed a man, I made sure to touch the charm in my apron pocket. Always it flicked and jerked and never rested. None of the men looked at me, though one or two greeted Grandmother.

"Am I ghost indeed, then, Grandmother?" I asked.

She gripped my hand. "It is fear of fairies. They will soon forget."

I nodded and held her hand tightly. Knowing that Death's dark realm lay just beyond the wood made my shabby little village seem bright. The crops in the fields had come up thick and fine, and in a day or so we would have rosy apples in the orchard. I felt affection for everyone I could see: Edwin Highfield cleaning his well, Mother Johnson limping from witch's shot, and the wagon master's son secretly holding hands with Mary Teacup there in the orchard. These were the same wattle-and-daub houses I had always known, the same climbing roses that adorned them. Surely I was safe, safe . . .

No, not safe. Compared with the forest, what was our village? What were our paltry shelters made from the bones of trees, our dingy fires that burned those bones alive, our obscene ash heaps? We hid in our hovels, pretending the forest was not all around us, though it sang while the ax gnawed at its edges. It grew and breathed and cast its long shadows. And yet—was there ever so beautiful a cathedral? Next to the forest, I realized, the chapel looked shrunken and slouched, and I knew I was not safe.

At the fire, boys and girls practiced footraces for the fair in the hopes of prizes of pull taffy. Men debated who might win first prize for the best cow or sheep or pig, defending the chances of others while secretly believing it would be their own that won. Women were making things to show and to sell: knitted things and lace and pretty bonnets and hose.

Everyone fell silent as I approached. Women who spun and knitted ceased their work. Most of the men looked down at their boots or gazed uncomfortably into the fire. Two or three looked at me challengingly. I knew from their looks that I would not be invited to tell a story tonight. Fairy tales were one thing, but another if they were real. I sat behind everyone, where I could feel none of the fire's heat.

No one told a story that night. The men talked of the harvest and their cattle, and the women of gardens and children, and Grandmother and I were the first to slip away for home. It seemed to me that Death's shadow had begun to separate me from my former life.

I was so tired that Grandmother had to slow her step for me on the uphill walk home. I dreaded the errand that still awaited me. Could I find the courage to walk again into the forest? I feared the answer was no.

I pretended to be busy while Grandmother readied for bed, but just when she was about to change into her night-clothes, a knock came. I jumped, but it was only Goody Thompson's nephew, calling Grandmother away on a mid-wife's errand. Grandmother bade me go to bed and assured me it would be quick.

"I will do this one without you, Keturah. You need your sleep. Besides, Goody's first baby took but an hour, and she scarcely needed me. The second will be quicker still."

No sooner had she gone than the wind began to roar in the forest and make the candlelight flicker.

I glanced out the window. The trees bowed to the wind. "Death," they breathed. "Our lord," they groaned as they bowed and swayed, at times elegantly and slowly, like a dance, and at times with great shaking and reeling, as if the branches wanted to flee from their roots in fear. I had to pay Soor Lily's price, but I could not bear to go into that forest. I had not found a true love, and Lord Death would know it.

Green leaves blew onto the windowpane and clung to it trembling, and the cow added her lowing to the din. I said a prayer for the little birds in the trees and for our chickens who roosted at the forest's edge, if they weren't already blown to Great Town. Somewhere in the village a shutter banged over and over, and beyond that, down at the pier, the boats knocked together. I sat, frozen on my bed, listening to the whistle of a stream of cold forest wind as it blew from a crack near the window. At times it was like the scream of a woman whose loved one is brought home lifeless, and at times like the whimpering of a child whose mother will never again come to him in the night. Again it sounded like the groaning of a man whose bed is empty and cold and whose wife will no longer work at his side. Now it sounded like a knock . . .

It was a knock indeed, and I realized that I had fallen, still sitting, into a half sleep.

I went to the door, my heart knocking louder than the din of the storm. It was Goody Thompson's nephew again. "Your grandmother bids you come to my aunt's bed," he said. His hair had been blown wildly against his face, and he panted as if he had run all the way up the hill. Yes, of course I would come.

I wrapped my shawl around me and followed the lad to Goody's house, grateful for an excuse to delay my errand.

Before I could enter the cottage, Grandmother came out. Her white hair blew around her face. She did not even try to hold down her skirts. "Go home, lad," she said to the boy, and he ran off, his jacket flapping in the wind like wings.

"Grandmother, I thought it would be over by now," I said.

She shook her head. "Goody is having trouble," Grandmother said.

"What can I do?"

"There is nothing either of us can do," she said.

"But you called for me."

"Not I, Keturah. Goody herself begged me to call for you." She examined my face closely. "Keturah, will you stay? Please."

"Stay?"

"Will you stay until the birth is over?"

"Yes, of course," I said.

"No matter how the birth goes?" Her voice sounded small against the roar of the wind.

"Grandmother, why are you asking me this?"

She took my hand in hers. "Keturah, when you were just a bit of a girl, I thought to train you in the midwife's art in case I died and left you with no means. And so you trundled along with me. At first you cleaned and cared for the littler ones. As you grew older, I taught you what I could."

"You have taught me well, Grandmother. You are a good midwife."

"I have lost three since you began coming with me. Before that, I lost none but your own mother. Do you remember the three, Keturah?"

I nodded and held my shawl close. The wind was so violent that the dark itself seemed to reach around me and howl. I said, "There was Melinda Stone, who died of triplets, and Jessica Cooper, who bled out. And June Siddal, whose daughter later cut her face. June's baby was breech."

Grandmother patted my hand. "You remember their

names. That is good. What else do you remember?"

I thought, trying not to hear the wind or feel it in my skirts. At last I said, "Nothing else, Grandmother."

"That is because you were not at any of those births, Keturah. Each time, you came into the house, looked about you a moment, and turned and left. The first time, with Melinda, you complained of a bellyache, and I thought nothing of it. The second time, with Jessica Cooper, you said the blood was making you faint. This from a girl who had helped with the hog slaughter since she was three. The last time, when it was June Siddal, you made no excuse, you asked no permission. You just left."

She stopped and placed her strong hands on my shoulders. "Keturah, I thought I was the only one who knew that you could see their deaths coming. But Goody Thompson knows too, somehow. I can do nothing more for her, though I pretend to busy myself. But she knows. She will be watching to see if you stay or leave. She is terrified to see what you will do. To see your death coming and to fear it—that is much worse than the dying. That is why I ask you to stay, no matter what."

I nodded slowly. "I will, Grandmother."

She hurried into the house, and I followed close behind.

But even as Grandmother spoke to me, I remembered something else from those birthings—that I had seen Lord Death before.

I had seen him that day when Grandmother fetched me to help Melinda's baby get born. There he was in the dimly lit room, comely and somber, yet comfortable, patient, as if he were a part of the family—a distant rich cousin, perhaps, or a well-traveled uncle. His face on the night of June's death, I remembered now, had been sad, and later so had our faces. The mother died, and the infant with her, and the poor woman's eldest daughter took a knife and cut her face so that she would never marry and have a baby.

I had seen him last year at St. Ivan's Feast, when the men had drunk too much ale and began to wrestle. There he had been a shadow among the men, tall, and with a lordly bearing. When I looked more closely, he was gone. The next day a man had been killed, and the blacksmith's son was gone. Poor Jenny Danson, for it was her father who had been killed, and her secret love who ran away.

I had seen Lord Death among us many times since I was a young girl, I realized now. Though I had not known who he was, as a child I feared him and hid my face in Grandmother's skirts if she would let me. As I got older, I came to believe that he had nothing to do with me.

He had been in the shadows, silent and pale. He hadn't looked at me or spoken to me, seemingly unaware that I could see him. Though I was young, I knew that I should not bring attention to his presence. I did not ask his name or point him out to anyone. I would see him standing, waiting patiently, respectfully. Though he was always there, I chose to ignore him, and I lived most days as if he were not often before me.

As I entered the Thompson house, I thought my fear screamed out, but instead it was Goody herself.

Her eyes fastened upon me the moment I opened the door, as did the eyes of Goody's mother and her sister, and of her husband holding their toddling child. Grandmother knew, and all these knew. The wind flung back the door, and I hastened to close it.

Once well inside, I looked at Goody with all the calm I could muster. I was aware of the low fire, and that Grandmother had cleaned the cottage and chased out the chickens, as was her wont, and that Lord Death stood in the shadows, his back to Goody.

"Will you stay then, Keturah?" Goody panted weakly.

Lord Death turned in a fluid, graceful motion and looked at me. In the forest he was tall and fine and strong, but here in a cottage he was royal and commanding, and his terrible beauty made the humble cottage shine with nobility.

Above the crackle of the settling fire, in a voice that only I could hear, and yet a voice that was piercing to my heart, he said, "Yes, Keturah, will you stay?"

"I will stay," I said to Goody. I sat in the willow rocker in the farthest corner of the cottage. I resolved that here I would sit, and I would not remove myself until the babe was born or the woman gone.

Goody's face crumpled into glad tears. "God bless you, Keturah," she said. Then the pains overtook her again.

Lord Death approached me, and as he did I could feel the heat of the fire less. I stopped rocking. His gleaming black boots reflected the dying coals of the fire.

"You are yet more beautiful by firelight," he said.

"It is only that I am not half-dead this time. Death is uglifying," I said pointedly.

"You were supposed to come," he said icily. "Did you not fear to incur my anger?"

"Why should I fear you now?" I said to him in a low voice, and yet fear filled my throat and my words quavered. The others, who had crowded around Goody's bed, could not hear me over the woman's moans. "I am not lost in your wood today."

"Yet now you see that you are safe nowhere," he said.

I said nothing.

After a time he said, "I did not know until now that you have always been able to see me, since you were a little child."

It angered me that he knew, and then I felt a certain relief, the kind that comes when a secret has been shared.

"Were you afraid, Keturah? When you were so young?"

"I thought you were a wealthy relative who never spoke, a high-born uncle, at first. Then came a day when I knew that to see you would mean someone would soon weep."

Goody Thompson thrashed in her bed and cried out. Grandmother commanded her in a sure and calming voice, and only I could detect the note of fear in it. Goody was drenched in sweat. Her lips were stretched white over her teeth. Her sister and her mother prayed aloud, and the tears rolled down Master Thompson's cheeks.

"How can you let her die?" I whispered.

He ran his hand through his hair. "Keturah, I would

have you know I take no pleasure in this. At least not this part of it."

Goody cried out again, and her boy in his father's arms began to sob. I was cold in spite of my wrap, but my heart was colder. "Then stop it," I said.

I realized that my words had fallen into a sudden quiet.

I saw that Goody's eyes were upon me in fear and crushed hope. "Death is here for me," she gasped. "You are speaking to him!" The pains overtook her again, and her little son cried out, "Mama!"

I pressed my hands together, but I could not keep them from shaking. "Can you hear her boy's pitiful cry? Can't you see she is needed?"

He looked at me sorrowfully. "She knows your secret certainly now. If she lives, they will tell it. It will not go well for you in the village."

The little boy's wails were more than I could bear. I stood. "For pity's sake, take the child to his aunt," I cried.

"Don't leave, Keturah!" Goody screamed.

"I won't," I said. "I won't!"

Goody's husband left as his son's wail freshened. He glanced pleadingly at me before the door closed on him. Goody screamed again. This time the fight had gone out of her pain, and there was nothing but the raw cries of one who works toward death.

"Please," I begged.

"It is better," he said.

"How could this be better?"

He was very still. Then he put his hand under my chin and lifted my face to his. I could not tell if the heat I felt was in my own face or from the burning cold in his fingers. At last he said, "Keturah, for your compassion, you shall have Goody's life. But you must come to me this night."

Over Goody's screams I could scarcely make out his words. "Her life," I said, "and—and the life of Soor Lily's baby son—and I will come."

He frowned and withdrew his hand. "He is no baby but a giant of a man. And he is destined for death. It is too late for him."

"Nevertheless," I said. I might have screamed it—I could no longer distinguish between my voice and Goody's. My lungs gasped for air as did hers.

Lord Death looked at Goody and back at me, then bent his head in assent. "You must keep your appointment with me," he said.

I nodded slowly.

Soon Grandmother called out, "The baby's head is coming, Goody, push, push!" and moments later, "A son—and as big as a calf."

I looked to see Lord Death, whether feeling gratitude or triumph I was not sure, but he was gone.

Goody's husband returned and cried harder even than his son had been crying, and everyone else, too, sobbed and laughed with joy. Goody had forgotten her pain already. Her eyes were full of her baby. I gazed at him, willing life into him, while Grandmother wrapped him and placed him in Goody's arms.

I glanced around Goody's small house. There was little in it but a bed and a pot or two, but she had picked fresh grasses to grace her window. I remembered that once when I visited her, she welcomed me as graciously as a queen might welcome a guest to her palace, and how I had envied her and her straw bed and her husband in it beside her, and her son too. Standing there now in the warmth of her joy and her home, I shivered to think of Lord Death's hand on my face. I gazed again upon the newborn, for it warmed me to do so, and meant to hold his tiny fingers, but Goody's husband blocked my hand. He shook his head. Grandmother, busy with Goody, did not notice.

When I opened the door to leave, Goody's husband came to see me out. "I thank you, Keturah, for my new son. But I bid you, come no more to my house again."

I could see in his face how much it had cost him to say this. "I will follow your bidding, sir," I said, and I left.

The sound of the midnight crows scraped against my heart as I made my way to the top of the village and toward the forest.

The oaks that rimmed the forest seemed to beckon with their long arms. "Come," they whispered, "come." But I knew that only a little way into the forest were brooding pines and towering elms. Dead brown needles crunched under my feet upon the path. I was afraid to veer off, knowing the tricks of trees.

I thought of turning back. With every step I thought of

it. But I knew I could not save my life by running away.

I stopped. There, off the path in a glimmer of moonbeam, was the great hart that had led me once almost to my death.

"And for all these many years Lord Temsland has not found you," I whispered. He was very still—not afraid of me, but wary. "No other stag has ever been able to elude the lord," I said softly, "for he is nothing if not a fine hunter. How . . . ?"

The hart lived ever in the shadow of the wood. He knew its winding ways, knew where to find its hidden brooks of water. When the forest's darker night fell upon him, then he rose up and led his herd to succulent herbs and fat nuts and sweet grasses. He lived side by side with death and was not sad.

"So that is why you escape Lord Temsland—Death has bargained with you too," I said. "But why?"

"Because," said a voice behind me, "he is so gloriously beautiful. Like you."

I turned to see Lord Death, and even in the dark I could tell that his eyes were upon me as if he had forever to consider me. I held my breath, waiting for him to seize me and take me away on his horse. But instead he leaned against a tree.

"Sir, we have plans to clean and repair the village, so the plague will not come." I was like a child who could not wait to tell her news. Me he might have, but he would not have my people. Not yet.

"Have you plans? Did I tell you that would help?" He sounded amused.

"No—but I inferred," I said.

"It will not be enough if Lord Temsland allows traffic with Great Town," he said bluntly. "There, the plague has already begun." He shifted to fit the curves of the tree he leaned against. "So—the end of the story, Keturah. Did the girl find her true love? Tell me the end of the story as you promised you would."

I had not thought about the ending of the story at all, so much had I been thinking of my own ending. I cast my mind about for a way to begin.

"Once there was a girl—"

"Ah, the saddest of endings."

"—who discovered Death's secret." Fear must be a fine storyteller, for I had no idea where these words had come from.

"This is not an ending but a beginning," he said.

"It is all part of the same story, sir."

He frowned. "This story is less believable than the first. But go on."

"His secret was . . . that though he was Death, and beyond all wanting, yet he wanted something, yearned and mourned and raged in his heart for something as only an immortal being can."

Lord Death had become very still. The trees around him were utterly silent, and even the air seemed to hold its breath. I too was silent for a moment, frightened, awed, to discover that this story was as true as the last.

"And what was it that Lord Death wanted and wept in his heart for?" I continued. "A love of his own, a consort to adorn his endless and hallowed halls, a companion who would comfort his heart when it broke from the sadness of his errands, who would weep with him when he carried home little ones in his arms, who would greet him with a joy equal to the terror with which mortals greeted him. Above all, he wished for a wife into whom he might pour his passion—"

"Hush. You try my patience," he said coldly.

But I did not, could not, stop. "But who would love such a one? What maid wished for gold coins to shut her eyes, or a satin-lined coffin for her marriage bed? What maid would come willingly? For he would have it be willingly."

The shadows that unfurled from his cloak had vanished, and his face caught the first light of the coming dawn, and he appeared no more than a man, no less than a great and warlike lord. I looked away, fearful that it might anger him that I saw him so vulnerable, so entranced by my story.

"And so he did his endless work," I continued quietly, "without feeling, without pity, without rest, for to open his heart to these would be to open his heart to his loneliness and longing, and that was beyond bearing."

"There are some who come willingly," he said quietly, as if he were afraid his own voice would break the spell of the story.

"There were some who came willingly," I said, as if I had not heard him, "not out of love, but out of sickness and sadness and a lack of understanding. He wanted none of them. And so he waited without waiting, and dreamed of what he could not imagine, and performed his terrible work and lived only in the moments out of which eternity is spun, knowing it was hopeless."

I stopped. The sun was almost up now, but Death had never been afraid of day.

"And then?" he asked.

I said nothing.

"And then!" he demanded.

"And because the girl knew his secret, she asked, 'Give me this day, and I will tell you the ending tomorrow.'"

I finished with closed eyes, for I felt his angry gaze as a cold in my bones, and I heard his icy breath come more quickly. I waited to feel his impatient touch, and to be swept into the heart of the still and ever-dark forest, never to return.

But the touch did not come.

I opened my eyes.

"For an ending to this story, I can pay a day," he said. "Come at day's end. And do not be late."

I stumbled home to my bed and, fearing the dark behind my eyes, fell asleep with my eyes open.

# VII

*An account of an invitation to the chamber
of John Temsland, which chapter is highly recommended
to the learning and edification of the
aforementioned blushing young maidens.*

*Plague.* It was my first thought upon waking. My second thought was of the touch of Lord Death last night. I could still feel his fingers under my chin, so close to my lips, where my breath was frozen.

I leapt from my bed and then sank back again, catching my breath. I remembered, then, my promise to come to Lord Death again tonight.

I held my hands before me. They trembled like an old woman's.

"You slept late, Keturah," Grandmother said tenderly. "Come, eat."

I willed myself to the breakfast table and ate what I could. I realized I had lost my sense of smell, and with it, my sense of taste. The porridge tasted like paste; the fruit was not what it had been the day before.

"Do they work on the road, Grandmother? I hear nothing."

"They began work on the road yesterday, Keturah,"

Grandmother said, patting my shaking hand. "They will surely begin again after chores." She made no reference to what had happened at Goody's in the night, but she was gentle with me.

"But the mill, Grandmother? Do they rid the mill of rats?"

Grandmother gazed out the window. "I see nothing from here."

I set down my spoon. "Tell me, Grandmother, do you see Soor Lily's baby son in the town?"

I closed my eyes and waited for her answer that seemed to come so slowly.

"Yes—yes, there he is, all brawny and fine. Why do you ask?"

"I—I heard he was unwell," I said, and I smiled. "Thank you for breakfast, Grandmother, and for letting me sleep."

She clucked and fussed with the dishes. "We must get you strong again in time for the fair."

Grandmother left to visit Goody Thompson and be sure that she and the baby were well, and I sat by the window gathering strength from the sunshine. A nightmare clung to me like cobwebs. I brushed at the place where Lord Death had touched me, where it tingled still. I wondered that he had given me another day. It made me not glad. Somehow I felt myself even more bound to him by it.

I willed myself to think of Ben Marshall and prize-winning pies. I would get the most finely ground flour today. I would make pies for practice until Tobias found my lemons. I would make a crust that would blow away when it was cut, and melted immediately upon the tongue. I would make a filling of fish and one of venison, one of strawberries and one of peaches. I would make a pie with potatoes and mushrooms and cheese in it, and another of plums. I washed myself shakily, summoned my strength, and made my way slowly to the mill for my flour.

As I walked, I saw that people were busy in their preparations for the fair. Men eyed one another's cattle and fed their own oats and apples. In their yards women made cheese and molded butters and sausages with highly guarded recipes. But no one yet worked on the road. The stones stood in piles like ancient grave markers.

Young women laughed together in companionable competition over their fair offerings and fell silent when I walked by. Martha Hornsby, who had always had a kind word for me, did not look up from her jam-making as I walked past her summer kitchen.

The young men, rather than working on the road or rat-ting the mill, were building booths for the fair. Some glanced up when I went by, but their eyes did not linger as they once used to do. Wherever I went, a wake of silence followed.

Lord Death had told me that if Goody Thompson lived, it would not go well for me with the villagers. He had been right. Their fear of death was greater than their sus-picion of fairies, it seemed. I did not dispute the fairness of their judgment. I knew what it was to think my heart safely nestled in its cage of bone, cradled in flesh, hidden and safe, and also what it was to suddenly and certainly know that Lord Death could reach his cold finger in and touch that heart, cause it pain, and still it. If I were friend to such a one, they thought, then I was no friend of theirs.

When I arrived at the mill, Miller said he was too busy to help me and made his apprentice do it, who trembled and got only half the flour into the sack.

"Barnabus Wren," I said impatiently, "why do you shake so? Have you seen a ghost?"

"No," he confessed, "but all the talk is that you have, Keturah. They say now that fairies didn't steal you, but that you were saved by Death himself—that is what Goody Thompson says, and her man does not deny it."

I looked at him a long moment. I did not even consider touching the charmed eye in my pocket. I could feel it moving even through my apron, my skirt, and my petticoat.

"That is *Lord* Death to you," I said at last, and left him standing open-mouthed.

When I arrived home with my flour, Gretta was there working her needle. She turned and looked at me sadly.

"They know," I said.

She said nothing.

"He warned me," I added as I set to work on the pastry.

"Then you have indeed seen him again?" Gretta asked.

I nodded.

"Were you afraid?" Gretta asked.

I nodded again. I was silent while I worked the fat into the flour.

Beatrice came in, gasping for air, having just run the entire way up the hill. "Chores are done—I must go sing, but oh, Keturah, God has not made me into a boy and—"

"God has answered your prayer, Beatrice," I said, and I fetched John Temsland's clothes and handed them to her.

"Oh! Oh, thank you, Keturah! How did you . . . ? Never mind, I don't want to know." She hugged me, and then held me away with her arms. "You are trembling, and so pale—"

"It is nothing," I said. "Dress. Go."

"It is true, then, what they are saying? That you spoke to . . . *him* last night?"

I nodded and eased myself into a chair and began working the pastry from a sitting position, the way I had seen Grandmother do of late. "I told him another story and again withheld the ending. He has given me another day. And with this day, God willing, I shall find my true love." I did not speak of my other object—I could not bear to frighten my friends with talk of the plague.

"Who will marry her, now that everyone knows?" Beatrice asked Gretta.

Gretta glared at her a moment, then looked at me sympathetically.

"Do they all hate me?" I asked.

"My family speaks for you," Gretta said.

"And mine," Beatrice said.

Gretta took a deep breath. "But they are afraid of you," she said, and Beatrice nodded.

"And Ben Marshall?"

"His mother has invited Padmoh to her home to teach her a kitchen trick or two."

"She wants Ben to marry Padmoh," I said.

"It might not mean that," Beatrice said soothingly.

"Young John Temsland laughs at the talk," Gretta said. "He says it is all tales and tattles, and besides, what could it hurt to have Death's dear in our own midst."

Again we all fell silent. I had added too much water and ruined the pastry. I put it in the pig's basket and began again.

After a time Gretta said, "You must go to Soor Lily."

"I have already gone to Soor Lily," I said.

"No!" Beatrice exclaimed.

Gretta said, "I have heard unsettling things about her."

"And yet she has warmed the heart of many a man to his lady," Beatrice said. Gretta gave Beatrice's arm a pinch.

"Look at Thermidor and Janie Lowfield," I said. "Thermidor hadn't a thought for Janie until Soor Lily gave her a charm. Now they are married and there was never a happier man."

"Nor a more miserable woman," Gretta said. Since I could not argue with her, I held my tongue.

"Beatrice, go," I said. "Choirmaster will be waiting for you."

She changed into the boys' clothing and stood before us shamefaced.

"Beatrice," I said, trying to summon a smile, "you will sing before the king, and surely you will win the king's shoe full of gold and a wish granted. Then you must use it as a dowry for your own true love, who might be Choirmaster himself."

Beatrice flushed and almost smiled, and then frowned. "I do not wish for a dowry," she said cheerfully. "What good is a dowry for one who would rather have angel wings than a husband? No, you shall have Choirmaster. If my singing pleases him, I shall use my influence to help him see how he must love you."

She turned to face the doorway, took a deep breath, and did not move. "Isn't this a sin, friends, to dress as a man?"

"Not if you are doing it for your friend. And for the king," Gretta said encouragingly.

"I admit I could desire to be of service to Lord Temsland," she said nobly.

"That is so like you," Gretta agreed.

Beatrice nodded and sighed deeply. "They say in countries across the sea that women sing in public. But here, of course, it is impossible."

I nodded. "There would be a scandal."

Beatrice took another deep breath and stared down the door. "Surely if a woman can cook for the king and a woman can sew to please the king, a woman can sing for the king."

"Like Tamara in the Bible, Beatrice," Gretta said, "sometimes a girl has to take extraordinary measures. That Keturah could find these clothes is proof that all is according to plan."

Beatrice seemed to contemplate the sinfulness of it all, but gradually her face filled with rapture. She drew her hands together as if she might pray.

"Yes, I see," she said in a tone that allowed me to hear the music in her voice. "It is all very clear now. We have had a miracle."

Face flushed, she ran out the door to choir practice. Once, exhilarated perhaps to be free of the skirts she had worn her whole life, she turned and waved to us and smiled joyfully. I smiled too. Even Choirmaster could not stay gloomy with Beatrice around, and I felt encouraged that Lord Death would be cheated of the man's soul if my plan worked.

Of course, there was still Tailor to worry over, but I had a plan for him as well.

⁂

Grandmother sent a message that she would spend the day with Goody Thompson, who would be bedridden for some time, and I made a potato and onion pie and then a raspberry pie while Gretta stitched. I wondered that though barrels of cobbles had been dumped in the square, no one yet had come to continue the work on the road. It made me taut as spun thread.

After a time there came a knock at the door. I jumped, and Gretta answered it.

It was Henry Bean, John Temsland's constant companion. He bowed to me. "Mistress Keturah Reeve," he said formally.

"You have known me since we were babies together, Henry," I said. "Come in."

"I am come on an errand from the young lord, John

Temsland. He is ready for the interview you have requested." Henry stepped away from the doorway and bowed again, gesturing grandly. "If you will allow me to escort you."

I remembered I had promised to return John's clothes, but they were at choir practice with Bill. There was no time.

I glanced back at Gretta, whose stitching had fallen into her lap. "I will be back shortly, Gretta," I said.

"Of course," she said.

I ignored Henry as I walked, thinking of how to tell John Temsland everything I must. In the middle of my musings I stopped, remembering suddenly the eye in my pocket.

I turned and waited for Henry to catch up with me. "Henry," I said.

"Yes, Keturah?"

"Henry, you have become a man almost," I said.

He smiled and puffed out his chest.

Could I love him? He was not handsome, but neither was he uncomely. He loved a good hunt and was not much for the fields. Still, it seemed he had become John Temsland's man, and whoever married him might have something more than a little peasant cottage.

"I have been a man for some time," he said proudly. "Why are you squinting at me?"

"Henry, could you love me?"

His mouth opened and shut with a snap. He took off his cap, ran his fingers through his hair, and put his cap back on. "Well, now, Keturah," he said uncomfortably, "'tis well known I have loved you since we played hide and seek as little ones together."

"But grown-up love, Henry? If I could summon up a love for you, could you return it?"

"Well . . . yes, I suppose I could," he stammered.

With great hope I touched the charm, but it was looking around, back and forth, up and down, more quickly than ever. I sighed. "Never mind, Henry. All is as it should be. A few days ago I didn't need my one true love. Now I do, but you are not it. Nor will you ever be."

I began walking again. Behind me, after a silence, Henry laughed a great laugh. "And pity the man who is," he said, throwing his arm around my shoulder. "Keturah, you have an angel on one shoulder and a devil on the other, and I don't know which I like more."

He led me to the manor and into John Temsland's chamber.

"Mistress Keturah Reeve," Henry said by way of introduction. After a bow to me, he left.

I stood just inside the entranceway of the chamber where John Temsland was looking through a window at his father's lands and people.

"I am sorry, sir, but I do not have your clothes," I began. It was best to tell him that first, I thought, before I spoke of the more important thing.

He seemed not to hear. He did not move or look at me when he said quietly, "The gossip is that when you leave a birthing, the mother dies."

I answered nothing.

"When you stay and attend, the mother lives, even if she should have died," he said.

"Who tells you this?" I asked.

"It is the talk of the whole village," John said. "Goody Thompson says she saw you conversing with an invisible being—an angel, say some; Death, says she. Some say that is why the fairies stole you into the wood and why they brought you back alive."

"Sir . . ."

"John."

"John, sir, if you are angry with me for the loss of your clothes, I can repay you in time. I will work in the kitchen—"

"You are welcome to the clothes, Keturah," he said, "though why you needed them I cannot imagine. All I ask is that you keep our secret about the hart."

"I will, sir—John."

"Keturah, I credit you with the grand idea of improving the village—building a road and freeing the mill of rats. Everyone credits you with the idea. And therein lies the problem."

"Problem?"

"Yesterday, when they thought you had only been stolen by fairies, they found you alarming, shall we say. They fear the fairies and their wild-wood magic, and they were nervous of one who had supposedly communed with them."

"I have seen no fairies, nor their enchanted halls," I said.

John turned away from the window and smiled kindly. "I believe you," he said. "But now this new tale—that is another thing altogether. No one has seen a fairy—'tis like there is no such thing. But all have seen Death's handiwork, and they all hate him, down to a man. Now they fear you with a fear that begets hatred, Keturah. The air around you, they think, is infected with death. They despise you because you remind them of their own mortality. The sight of you bodes their own end."

I looked at my feet.

"That leads me to the problem, Keturah. You see, because it was your idea to build the road, they will no longer do it. They—they believe that you are on Death's errand."

I looked up at him in alarm. "But it is just the opposite!" I cried.

He studied me a few moments and then gestured to a chair. "Sit, Keturah. You are trembling."

Gratefully, I sat down. "Sir, I would tell you my story, but you would not believe me."

"My name is John, and I will believe you, Keturah." His eyes were full upon me. Every bit of him seemed willing to listen.

"But you don't know me. How will you believe the tale I am about to tell?"

"I've known you for almost your whole life. I've listened to you tell stories around the common fire, and watched how even as a young girl you captivated your listeners."

"But—but you were never there."

"Ah, but I was. Hiding nearby, in the shadows where no one could see," he said.

I remembered him as a young lad, always on the edge of

village activities. He played football with the boys, but was not allowed to join in the festivities of the winning team afterward. He helped in the fields, but went to the manor after the planting and harvest instead of joining our feasts. When the other boys played, John learned to read and do sums. While the other boys fished, John learned archery and hunting. He must always have been lonely, it occurred to me now, and I could well imagine him listening to our stories but never coming into the circle.

"You should have come and warmed yourself. We would have made you welcome," I said.

He bent his head thoughtfully. "Keturah, you see for yourself how difficult it can be to be accepted into a circle of people who consider you to be different."

"Yes," I said.

He waited silently while I tried to gather my thoughts. I would be telling a story more far-fetched than any I had told before, and yet it would be true.

"I followed the hart into the wood that day I was lost," I began. "How many tales had I spun of the hart, and here he was before my eyes, as if my words had summoned him. Like the truth in a story, he eluded me until he nearly destroyed me, and then when there was no going back, he left me in the dark of the wood.

"The fairies that I never saw nor heard must have laughed me to scorn. I wandered and wandered, and the bugs bit and the underbrush tripped my feet and the night winds froze me. Then Death himself came to collect me.

"I used the only means I could think of to postpone the

114

inevitable—I told him a story. A love story. And I agreed to tell him the rest of the story the next night, if only he would let me live another day.

"And so he did. I told him that the love story was true, that it was my story."

I stopped. John hunkered down beside my chair. His eyes were on the same level as mine, and they mirrored the images in my mind. I thought I had never seen such a beautiful young man. My hand crept to my apron pocket, and then stopped. It was absurd—I was a commoner, and he a lord's son. I forced my thoughts back to my errand.

"While we were talking, he offered to let another die in my place. He said it would scarcely matter whom I chose. Many will die of the plague, he said, and when I pleaded with him to tell me how to stop it, he said, 'It is not in your power—your manored lord has allowed his lands to fall to dire ruin.'

"So you see, sir, John, why I spoke up after the king's messenger left. I saw the king's visit as an opportunity to waylay the plague. We must have the road, and the rats in the mill must go. And there must be no traffic with Great Town."

After a long moment, John nodded. I could see that his horror at the threat of plague was equal to my own.

"You must speak to the villagers, tell them about the coming plague, Keturah," John said after some thought. "Perhaps then they will resume work on the road."

"Do you think they will believe me?"

"Oh, they will believe you," he said with conviction. "Haven't they always believed your fairy tales? Didn't all your stories of the great hart produce a real hart, Keturah? They will believe you."

I stood up. "Then I must try."

# VIII

*Soor Lily and I concur; Ben brings a squash;*
*the arrival of Tobias with lemons that disappoint;*
*and I cook pies.*

Henry quickly spread the word that John Temsland would address his people in the village square, and just as quickly the people began to gather.

The sun was hot, and no breeze blew in from the bay, and soon people were grumbling and miserable. How had half the day gone by, I wondered. I willed time to slow. John led me to the square and climbed to the top of a pile of cobblestones.

"My people," he said, his arms toward them. "I stand on these stones that should by now be laid over the square. But no one came to the work today. Would you not have the king come and see that our village is everything my father said it was?"

"There is still much left to harvest, young John," said George Puddington. "We have our own work to do."

"Will the leavings of the harvest not wait until after the fair, George?" John countered.

George cast a sullen look at me and said nothing.

"We have the bay, and the forest for hunting," Peter Whitty called. "We are not ashamed of Tide-by-Rood."

"But why do you object to making it even better?" John said, smiling, cajoling.

"We are tired at the end of the day," Peter replied. The crowd murmured in agreement.

"Peter, George, all of you—did you stop to think why the great lords have put it in the king's mind to come to Tide-by-Rood at this time, and on such short notice? They don't like my father, who advises the king to be merciful and kind to the commoners. He tells the king that his power comes to him because of the people's love. The great lords want to oppress the people, assert even greater authority, and so they wish to have my father shamed, to take him further out of favor with the king. Perhaps they will take away his lands and a new lord will come, one who would be less kind to you than my father has been."

The crowd murmured.

"What has she to do with you, John?" Peter asked, pointing at me. "Has she cast fairy dust in your eyes? Or worse?"

"If loyalty to my father is not reason enough, then Keturah Reeve has something to tell you," John replied. "I adjure you to listen to her."

Only a few days before, men had looked on me with soft eyes. Now they were reluctant, suspicious, hard.

"She is why we stopped work on the road," Paul Stoppish called out. "It was her idea first, wasn't it?"

Others joined in. "Who told you to speak up about the road, Keturah? Was it Death, wishing to see us perish from heat and fatigue?" a voice called out. "Will he send down a stone on the head of an unsuspecting one?" cried another. "Will a hammer break and kill him who wields it?" shouted Patsy Krundle in front.

John held up his hand to silence them. "Listen to her, I tell you." He reached down and lifted me up onto the stone pile. I was trembling so that I could scarcely focus my vision upon the crowd. I opened my mouth to speak, but I did not know how to begin.

John encouraged me with a kind look.

I cleared my throat and took a breath, and still no words came to mind.

John put his hand on my back and faced the crowd. The sun seemed to have burned the air—it had a smoky, acrid smell to it—but no one moved or murmured.

"The rumors you have heard are true. Keturah has seen Death, and she has learned something that we all should know. Speak, Keturah. Tell them—"

"—that plague comes," came a voice from the crowd. There was a cry and an intake of breath from the villagers, and all eyes turned to Soor Lily, for it was she who had spoken. Six of her seven sons hovered protectively around her. The seventh, I noticed suddenly, was standing guard by me at the base of the stones.

She walked to the front of the crowd where everyone could see her.

"Plague—in Angleland," she said. "I can smell it. I've known for some time."

The crowd erupted with shouts and cries.

"Please!" John said.

"You cannot run—there is nowhere to go," Soor Lily cried.

The crowd became quieter. Though they feared her for a witch, still there was not one in the crowd who had not been helped by her—with the toothache, the bellyache, or the earache, with lumps or festers or ulcers or malaise.

"It is a way off, but not so far it could not find us. We should listen to what she has to say," Soor Lily said, and she turned to me, waiting for me to speak.

Gretta and Beatrice joined the crowd. I saw Gretta nod at me as if to say, "Speak, friend."

"Death treads less easily where there is a good road," I said, and though my voice was cramped, it carried in the quiet. I raised my voice. "Death does not dwell in clean corners and hates nothing more than a sludged well and a mill with no vermin. If you will bring neatness and order, perhaps—perhaps the plague will not come. If we can work together, and the strong help the weak, and if we share the burden, surely . . ."

But some part of me knew, even as I spoke, that Lord Death, clean as a filed blade as he was, did not always want the souls we so willy-nilly sent to him. I wondered if he had put the thought in my mind, or if mere proximity to him was teaching me.

"And no one must go to Great Town," I added.

As I spoke, the eyes of the men got larger, as if their ears were not big enough to hear what I was saying and their eyes had to help.

"I believe her," said Henry Bean's father, Caleb.

"And I," said Gretta's father, Will.

"We must work on the road all night," said Beatrice's father, James.

A few wives were wheedling their husbands into submission. Mothers hugged their children close and hurried them back to home.

John jumped down and the men gathered, and before I could get entirely away, work on the road had begun.

I headed for home, for I was weary, weary. I had not gone far when I was stopped short by something splattering at my feet—a rotten apple. I was too tired even to look for the culprit. I stepped over it, and another landed nearby. This time I stopped and looked behind me. John Temsland was coming toward me, and in each hand was the ear of an attached boy. They squirmed and came with their ears.

"These boys have somewhat to say," John said cheerfully.

"Sorry," squeaked one boy.

"Sorry," said the other.

John let them go, and they ran away, rubbing their ears. "I will have a man watch over your house," he said.

"I am not afraid," I said. Not of *them*, I added in my thoughts. Against the one I truly feared, no one could guard.

I bent my head in respect and continued on my way.

"You are a brave woman, Keturah Reeve," he called after me.

I scarcely heard him, for the sun was on its descent, and my mind reeled for a new story.

When I arrived home, Grandmother placed dinner before me with a loving pat. After, I washed the wooden platters and the horn mugs, and placed them neatly on the shelf under the cooking table next to Grandmother's steel and flint. While devising every possible story, I made sure all the wooden spoons were face down to keep out the devil, as Grandmother had instructed me since I was a baby. I was sweeping the floor, and had almost grasped an idea for the story I must tell Lord Death, when who should come but Ben Marshall.

"I thought you were very brave today," Ben said timidly. "I brought you this." He handed me a purple squash.

I thanked him and cradled the squash in one arm like a baby. With the other hand I reached into my apron pocket and discovered to my dismay that the eye had not stopped and was rolling up and down and side to side as before.

"I never believed that you were stolen by the fairies," he said quietly.

"No, Ben, it was not true," I said. I had paid the price—why didn't it stop? The squash was evidence that he was smitten with me.

He cleared his throat. "There is much talk. Mother has heard it. But all the talk in the village can't stop you from winning Best Cook at the fair. Isn't that so, Keturah?"

I squinted at him, forcing my eyes to think him the most beautiful of men. I willed myself to love him. *Love him!* I commanded my heart. But the eye continued to roll.

Grandmother came in from the garden and seemed delighted to see I had a visitor. "What news, Ben?"

"Good day, Grandmother Reeve. I—I just came to tell you that the poor parish priest's cow died of the bloat," Ben said.

"Perhaps he should have sprinkled his cow with stolen holy water like Farmer Dan," Grandmother said, chuckling.

"I heard Dan tell the priest his flock had grown so fat, it was hard to repent," Ben answered. It was clear he was trying to charm her. "The priest said his flock might become so holy they would refuse to mate. That put the fear into him." Grandmother laughed and Ben blushed at his own joke.

It was a good joke, I thought as they continued to talk. Grandmother thought it funny. Why didn't I? I had tried to laugh, but it came out more like a hiccup. Surely the eye was only waiting to see if I would win Best Cook.

"Ben," I said, interrupting a lengthy speech on the fine art of growing asparagus, "would you come tomorrow to try my pies?" If only there would be a tomorrow.

He smiled. "Of course, Keturah. It is good that you are practicing your cooking for the fair."

"Ben, what if I don't win Best Cook?" I said.

"You must win, Keturah," Ben said. "I am bound by tradition."

"Yes," his mother said, startling us both by appearing in the doorway. "Tradition."

"Constance," said Grandmother. "Won't you come in?"

"I will not," she said. "And Ben is needed at home."

"Constance, surely you don't believe the . . . the talk," Grandmother said stiffly.

"We don't want your fairies in our garden," Constance said shortly. "They eat holes in the chard and make webs between the beanstalks."

"Mother!" Ben said.

"Mother Marshall, I assure you I have had no dealings with fairies," I said.

"No? Then is it true that it is worse than fairies, that you have had dealings with *him?*"

"Mother, please. Go—I will follow shortly," Ben said.

His mother gave me a sour look and turned to leave. When she was down the path, Ben said, "Keturah, I am bound by the Marshall tradition to marry the Best Cook, but I am also freed by it. Win Best Cook, and no one, including Mother, can nay-say it."

He smiled a wide smile and followed his mother down the path. Though it was the handsomest of smiles, the eye continued to roll and my heart was unmoved.

Never mind. I would train my heart to love Ben and his baby-sized purple squashes. And when I won Best Cook, the eye must be still.

"Goodbye, Ben," I called after him. "Thank you for the beautiful squash."

⊷∢⊷

For the rest of the day and on into the night, I listened to the ringing of hammers and the shouts of men as they worked on the road, and I practiced pies. Gretta and

Beatrice came, and I plied them with pie. They assured me that my pies were the best in the village, but I knew they would have to be wondrous to win Best Cook. I made the pies I had dreamed of: one of fish, and one of venison; a strawberry pie, and a peach, and a plum; and one of potatoes and mushrooms and cheese—and all with a crust that almost blew away when it was cut.

That evening, as I prepared to take samplings of my pies to Cook, I watched the sun set in a green sky and plotted the story that would save my life. Gretta stitched by the fire, and Beatrice practiced her arpeggios and chatted with Grandmother.

A laurel-leaf willow tree that grew at the very edge of the forest, and had been growing beyond its bounds for some time, brushed up against the window as the evening breeze came on. One slim bough tapped with the wind.

Knowing that it was a harmless tree did not lift my heart at all. All day long our cottage seemed to hunch away from the shadow of the forest, and now that shadow encroached boldly upon it, almost touching it. Would that Grandfather were still alive and still able to take his ax to the trees that stole slowly into our little plot of land.

Then a face appeared at the window, and my heart pounded hugely in my chest, like the thump of a great empty drum, until I realized it was our cow, Bridie. She always huddled close to the house as night fell.

A knock at the door startled Bridie away.

"Who could that be?" Grandmother asked.

At the door, to my relief, was Tobias, and in his hands

a small burlap bag. He was flushed and dirty, and behind him his horse was lathered.

"My lemons!" I exclaimed. "Did you get my lemons, Tobias?"

"I did," he said. "The most beautifulest round lemons you ever saw."

I tore the little burlap sack out of his hands. "Round? But Cook said they were ovals. Like eggs laid by the sun, she said." Gently I eased the fruit from the sack onto the table.

Tobias grinned. I stared. Behind me everyone gathered and craned their necks to see.

"Ah," said Gretta, "you have done it now, Tobias."

"Yes," Tobias said proudly.

"Tobias," Gretta said, pinching her brother by the ear, "what color is the sun?"

"Why, it is yellow, Gretta," said he, wincing.

"Tobias, what color is a dandelion?" she asked, tugging on Tobias's ear.

"As yellow as the sun, Gretta," Tobias said, grimacing.

I had not breathed one breath since I saw the fruit.

"Keturah," Beatrice said finally, "why are your yellow lemons so . . . orange?"

"It is because they are oranges, and not lemons," Gretta said, yanking Tobias's ear. I stayed her hand.

Tobias began backing away. "But—but the man said they were lemons, or as good as. Sweeter, he said."

"Go back, Tobias," Gretta said. "Go back and get lemons. Yellow—*yellow!*—lemons!" She chased him out of the kitchen and threw two of the oranges at him.

I ran after him. "Tobias!" I called. "Tobias! Stop!"

He stopped, panting, and regarded me cautiously, as if I might try to pelt him with fruit.

"Have them!" I said. "Surely after your long journey you at least deserve to eat some."

He gazed longingly at the oranges. "I was tempted many times," he said, "but I didn't want to eat even one of your . . . lemons." He sighed and ran a hand through his hair. "How was I to know, Keturah? Have I ever seen a lemon before? Or an orange, for that matter?"

"Come, Tobias, come in. Rest yourself," I said. "Come, I have been cooking pie."

He followed me into the house dejectedly, and Grandmother served him. Gretta scowled at him, and Beatrice sniffed often and refused to look at him.

"When I am done, I shall go again to seek out lemons for you," he said.

"Never mind, Tobias—only if you can."

"Of course he will," Gretta said. "And not just for Keturah, but for John Temsland and the queen."

Tobias nodded, determined.

"You must not go to Great Town, Tobias," I said, "for fear of the plague."

Beatrice patted his hand. She had already forgiven him for orange lemons.

⌖

When Tobias left, I realized with a start that the forest shadows touched the cottage.

No. I could not make myself go. Not yet. Didn't I have to take samples of my pies to Cook for her opinion? Surely he could wait. Surely he had forgotten about me, busy as he must be, escorting popes and peasants and emperors to their doom.

I put a large piece of each pie on a tray, went out into the evening, and fastened my eye upon the cookhouse where Cook slept in a tiny side room. Cook must taste my pies now and tell me which one would win me the prize. She would be angry with me for waking her, for she was always early abed, but wake she must, for Ben Marshall must love me, and must marry me, Best Cook of the fair.

True, I did not see in him my one true love as yet, and the charm's eye did not stop for him, but that could change at any moment. I felt a pang of regret that Padmoh, who wanted him too, should have to fail in her objective if I succeeded. But I consoled myself that her interest was the man's garden and not the man himself.

I was halfway between my home and the cookhouse when a mist of cloud began to creep across the early-risen moon. It darkened the ground enough that I did not see a small depression, and I stumbled. Immediately I was steadied by some force I could not see, and then, as if the coming night clotted into a visible personage, I perceived that Lord Death was beside me.

We walked together in silence for a time, and then I said humbly, "Sir, I was going to come, truly."

"And you shall come," he answered, "but I thought to remind you."

His lips seemed very close to my ear, but I did not look at him.

His cloak billowed out behind him and brought the full night. He made no effort to touch me, but I felt beside me a man. I looked up at his face, severe and handsome, and saw sorrow stretched along the lines of it.

"I believe I will not stay with you tonight, Lord Death," I said softly. Could he hear the doubt in my voice?

He made a small bow and was silent.

"What does it feel like to die, sir?" I asked. "It hurts—I know only that."

We walked for some time in silence. At last he said, "It is life that hurts you, not death."

I shivered to think of the green-black night in the forest, and said, "My lord, why do you trouble me by walking with me in the dark? It is cruel."

"I think to protect you from them," he said.

And then, without turning my head, I saw the black shadows of men against the blue-black night. They were watching me, and still, and silent.

"It is gallant of you, sir," I said softly, "but I am more wishing of their company than yours. And it is your company, after all, that makes them fear me and hate me."

He said nothing. I was almost there . . .

I ran the final steps to Cook's house and pounded on her door. "Cook!" I cried. I pounded again. "Cook!"

I could hear her cursing within, and then she swung the door open. She was dressed in her nightclothes and wore a woolen nightcap on her head.

"What is it? What? Has the moon fallen out the sky?"

"Cook, you must taste my pies!" I said. I glanced behind me to see nothing but moon-washed dark, and slipped into her kitchen.

She stood speechless, perhaps for the first time in her life. I picked up a piece of pie and shoved it at her. "Eat," I said, "and tell me if I will win Best Cook."

She took the pie and said, "You are mad, but they say mad cooks make the best sauce."

Cook chewed and tasted each pie once, twice, thrice. At last she spoke.

"Keturah, you make the best pies I have ever tasted, but every woman in the village can make pies of this variety. If you want to win Best Cook, you will need to make a new kind of pie, one that will make every woman clamor for your recipe."

"Tobias says he will find me lemons."

"Do so, and Ben Marshall will be yours. If you want him." She peered at me and wiped her mouth with her apron. "Are you sure you want him?"

"And why should I not?"

"Because he wants a cook, not a true love, and you want a true love."

I drew in my breath. "How—how did you know?"

"John Temsland told me so."

I stared at her in her nightgown and apron. "John Temsland spoke of me to you?"

"He did." She gazed at me sideways with her eye that

still had some short vision in it. "He mentioned you more than once."

I was helpless to think of a reply, and attributed my lack to fatigue. "I must go home," I said at last.

"Wait."

She woke her son, insisting that he accompany me home. The poor man grudgingly complied, and was so sleepy he saw neither my more powerful escort nor the men who watched me in the shadows.

Within sight of the cottage, Cook's son turned back, crossing himself as he did so.

# IX

Another story;
the extraordinary price Soor Lily exacts
for a little of her foxglove and which price I pay in full,
though not without the deepest trepidation.

The stars had come out again.

I had heard tales of scholars who said the stars were really great suns, but so far away they appeared as pinpoints of light. Everyone knew that it was impossible and laughed at the scholars.

But now, as I gazed upward, I hoped it was true—hoped that the cold, empty sky could be filled with such heat and light, that the universe could be something impossible, something beyond my eyes and imagination, something unholdable.

No, I could not leave these stars just yet. I entered the cottage.

The fire was low. "Grandmother?" I called. She was not in her bed. And then I saw that she was lying on the floor.

"Grandmother!" I went to her side. She was awake but pale as a candle, and there was a film of sweat on her forehead and upper lip. "Grandmother?"

"Keturah, I'm glad you've come," she said quietly.

"You are ill!" I said.

"Help me to my bed."

Slowly I helped her to her bed and covered her well.

She settled under the quilts, and I took her hand. It shook in mine like a captured bird. "I am afraid, Keturah."

"Grandmother, I will protect you," I said.

She glanced all about the room, fear in her eyes. "Do you see him, Keturah? Is he close?"

"No, Grandmother, he is not close."

I gripped her hand with both of mine.

"Grandmother, wouldn't I tell you if he were near?" I said gently. "All is well. Here, let me brush your hair."

"Keturah," she said with weary surprise. "I am dying."

"No, Grandmother," I said.

She looked at me long in silence.

"No," I said again, more firmly.

"Will you let me die alone?" she asked.

Angrily I said, "Grandmother, it is only the ague, that which vexed you last winter."

She frowned slightly and gazed out the window. "It is not truly death I fear. It is leaving you behind. As long as I am alive, the memory of your revered grandfather protects us. As long as I am alive, Lord Temsland remembers to give us a small pension. But when I am gone, you are alone. You will be vulnerable when the reputation of your grandfather dies with me."

"Do not fear, Grandmother," I said. "Sleep now."

I unwound her braid that fell to the floor and brushed her hair, smooth as silver silk. Then I began to plait her hair again. It felt warm and comforting to have my hands in her hair, as when I was a little child. At last she fell asleep, but she seemed at times to forget to breathe, and she slept terrifyingly still.

I left her then and ran into the forest, black and dark as a nightmare. He was waiting for me, his horse, Night, beside him. "Do you think by flaunting your power you will make me love you?" I cried when I saw him, rage killing my fear.

He stood tall, composed, lordly. "Your grandmother is very ill, Keturah," he said calmly. "I told you she would die soon. I told you in the forest when you were lost. It has begun."

It was true that he'd told me this, but it made no difference. Warning made no difference. "Why must you hide in shadows? Why am I the only one who sees you? Are you a coward?" Oh, how good it felt to rail against him.

"I am here for all to see, Keturah, if they wish it," he said, still calm. "I have touched them all in some way." He stepped closer to me. His tone had an edge to it now. "They think my realm is far away. Would they sleep at night if they knew how close I was? Would they sing so roundly by the fire if they knew I was waiting in their cold beds? Would they be so glad of the harvest if they knew I rested in their root cellar? It is not I who am the coward."

He stepped closer again to me. His limbs were powerful, graceful, his movements almost a dance.

"Not at all, sir," I said, matching my tone to his. If I must lose Grandmother to him, I would not do so in silence. "They know what you are, and that you are near.

We all know you. When it is winter and we must walk in the blizzard snow, do not our fingers and toes whisper death? And when winter is at last over but the potatoes are gone and the bacon is moldy, can we not hear our bellies whisper death to us? In the dark, don't we know? And when we are paralyzed by nightmares? We know what you are. With our first cries we rail against you. We see you in every drop of blood, in every tear. No wonder they hate me for communing with you."

He took another step toward me. "The story," he said. "That is all I care to hear from you. Now there are two stories, and two endings, and I shall have them both, Keturah. My patience is spent."

Yes, the story, I thought. With the story I would take my revenge upon him.

"And then one day," I said fiercely, "Death did find love." Of course, I thought—there could be no other ending.

"But you said it was hopeless," he protested.

"It was hopeless, but in story, all things can be."

"I don't believe it. This is a most unsatisfactory ending."

"That's because it is not the ending."

"What? Another beginning?"

"Death found his love, but the object of his undying love did not return his affections."

"Astonishing," he murmured wryly.

"He watched her all her life, watched her grow up, watched her become more beautiful by the day, and watched her become a woman. He listened by the common fire, in the deep of the shadows, as she told tales. And he loved her more every day. She paid him no attention, and lived her life as if he were invisible and not real at all. He sought a way to make his true love see that she was his lady, his queen, his consort. Desperately he examined every means—he could abduct her, but he wanted her willing. And so he lured her into the forest, and all but killed her, and then arranged to have her come to him each night to weave him a tale."

I stopped, but he was utterly silent, utterly still.

And then he laughed—a great, deep, echoing laugh that made the branches lash as if startled and the black stallion shy and whinny. He raised his arms and spun in his high black boots and laughed again, and his laugh rang into the forest as if he would laugh all the trees down.

And then the mirth left his face and he said, "I will not hear this tale anymore. I will hear the tale of the girl. What of her, Keturah?"

I hugged my arms. How foolish to think that anger and cruelty and revenge could hurt Death. I began to shiver. Please, I begged in my heart. *Please . . .*

"Once there was a girl—who guessed Death's secret . . . and she asked him—asked him for her grandmother's life, knowing that he loved her."

"And in this story," Death asked, "what did he do?"

"He granted her this wish because—because she was the one he loved."

The wind spun around me. Leaf dust stung my eyes and choked me. But Lord Death was not touched by the wind. All about him was still.

"And did she return his love?" he asked quietly.

"Ah, that," I said most quietly, for the heart had gone out of me, "that is the ending, and I cannot tell it until tomorrow."

After a long silence, he said, "Go. Your grandmother sleeps a healing sleep. In the morning, give her foxglove tea. I will see you tomorrow. Do not be late. And Keturah, I warn you—never ask again."

It took me a moment to realize that he had given me hope. I looked up to thank him, but he had gone.

I ran through the black forest until I arrived home, where the candles guttered in the windowsills and the coals breathed in sleep.

I knelt by grandmother, vigilant until the sun paled the sky. By morning light I could see that the gray was gone from her face, and I left to go to Soor Lily's.

When I opened my door, I saw that down in the village center below, the men and boys and women were already at work. The people sang and laughed as they worked on the road, and young John Temsland went from group to group upon his horse. Each group cheered him as he approached, and he encouraged them with words of praise, and dismounted to add his own strength to whatever task was at hand. Some of the cottages sparkled gaily with new whitewash, and the boats bobbed brightly with new coats of paint.

Jenny Talbot, a young girl who often walked with her pet pig at the edges of the forest so that it might find acorns, was close by our cottage. Her pet had become the most enormous pig in the village, but her father did not have the heart to slaughter it because of his daughter's love for the creature.

I stopped, unseen, to watch her for a moment. She chattered sweetly to the animal, and sometimes she picked up acorns and fed him. Occasionally the pig raised its head, seemingly to listen to her, and picked the acorns delicately out of the palm of her hand.

How had I never noticed before how dear she was? How dear, in fact, was everyone in my village, and every house and tree and garden. How comforting the whisper of the wheel of the mill, the clanging of the smith's hammer, the lowing of cattle, the laughter of women. Were there any jewels so beautiful as the apples in the orchard, any decoration more lovely than the flowers that grew around every cottage and sprouted in the thatch of their roofs and tumbled over arbors?

Jenny saw me then, and curtseyed.

"Jenny," I said, "why do you curtsey when I am in no station above you?"

"I thought to cry out, and then curtseyed instead," Jenny said. "They say you are a witch who covens with Death."

"You must not believe everything that is said, Jenny. The poor fortunes that brought me close to Death have made me love life no less. Come now, tell me, is that not a new frock you are wearing, Jenny? It is the same green as your eyes."

"Yes, and I have another that makes my eyes blue," she said, "but I may not wear it until fair time."

"How do you come to have two new frocks?" I asked.

Jenny's was one of the poorer families in Tide-by-Road.

"Lady Temsland has given cloth stuff to every family in the village. She says if a clean and pretty village will keep death away a time, as you say, perhaps clean and pretty people will keep him away longer still."

Surprised as I was, there was no time to think of a reply, for I felt an urgency to get to Soor Lily's for foxglove for Grandmother.

"Goodbye, then, Jenny of the changeable eyes," I said.

"Goodbye, beautiful witch Keturah," she said ever so politely.

As I walked down toward the village square, I saw that fresh-washed linens hung on the lines. Honey Bilford was firing her pothook, and her neighbor was sweeping out her root cellar. Young men polished their spades, sharpened their axes, and oiled the yokes. Young women scoured crock and kettle until they could see their pretty faces in them. Down by the water, some of the men were repairing the pier, and Andy Mersey was carving a beautiful sign that said "Welcome to Tide-by-Rood." The church bell shone like gold.

I met the cobbling crew along the way, and in the middle of them was John Temsland. Someone told him of my approach, and he straightened. The men drew away, scowling and muttering, but at a word from John they all doffed their hats.

"Keturah, what think you?" John said. "By tomorrow, one will be able to walk to every house in the village without muddying his feet. The women have been just as busy as the men. There isn't an untidy cupboard or a dirty corner in any cottage of the village. Mother has got the manor fitted as royally as she can, too."

"You have all done well," I said.

"It was your counsel that inspired us, Keturah Reeve," John said.

I blushed and said, "I must be on my way. Grandmother is poorly."

He stepped aside with a slight bow, and I hurried up the path.

"If I may, I will pay my respects to your grandmother later," he called after me. I nodded my head in quick assent, and continued on.

The thatch was being freshened on every cottage roof, and girls were lining the pathways with whitewashed stones. The door and shutters of one cottage had been painted an apple green, and those of other cottages were yellow, a bright blue, and lavender. Rosebushes had been pruned and barrel irons polished. People worked and laughed, but when I walked by they looked away, and no one spoke to me.

I could not guess what price Soor Lily would ask for fox-glove, but whatever it was, I set my mind to pay it. Walking on the cobblestones eased the fatigue in my bones.

The wise woman was standing at the door when I arrived, as if she had been apprised of my coming. I could see two of her sons hiding in the bushes to the side of the house.

Soor Lily seemed more solicitous than before, more hoveringly nervous. She set tea before me so carefully the bowl made no sound as it touched the table.

"Keturah," she said, "it is not enough, is it? The road,

the mill—they will not be enough, perhaps."

"I don't know . . . Yes, of course they will . . ."

"You are not well. See how pale you are, and how your hands tremble, and you are wasting. So thin."

"I am fine. I didn't sleep well. I—I have come for Grandmother, Soor Lily. Please, I need foxglove."

"Foxglove, yes. I have foxglove for those who fear to find it for themselves."

"Please," I said. "I will have some. For Grandmother."

"For your dear grandmother. She has always been kind to me."

Soor Lily arose and fetched foxglove, bringing me a folded paper of crushed leaves.

I went to take it, but she snatched it back so quickly and so deftly that it vanished, leaving me wondering if she had really held it out to me at all.

"Please, Soor Lily. I have no money," I said, my voice trembling in spite of my intention to be firm. "I've nothing more to give you. If I ask even the smallest favor of Lord Death again, I will most certainly die."

"No, no. It is just foxglove, pickable for anyone who looks. No, sweetums. This is but a small thing, this foxglove, and so I ask only a small favor of you." She stroked the foxglove thoughtfully. "Look at my sons while touching the charm."

I was speechless.

"It is a nothing price, yes?" she said quietly, nodding.

When I remained silent, she went to the door and the window, and one by one her sons assembled. The room that was so roomy now became stiflingly small as the seven men trooped in, hunched and pouting like little boys caught in a misdeed.

Soor Lily placed the foxglove on the table. I gazed at it for strength to do what was required, and then, slowly, I reached my hand into my apron pocket and touched the charm.

One son folded his arms tightly, seemingly angry that he must be looked at. One, the baby whom Lord Death had allowed to live, looked frightened and bit his fingernails. One was pigeon-toed. Another picked at his ears, and still another breathed through his mouth, allowing spittle to collect at the corners of his lips. The other two hid behind their five brothers so I could barely see them.

Soor Lily put her mouth close to my ear. "Hold the charm now, sweetums," she said. "Look at my darlings. That is the price I ask for foxglove—to look. Is that not the smallest of fees? Only look."

For a moment I thought of grabbing the foxglove and running, but I knew I would never be able to run through that wall of men.

I gritted my teeth and held the charm while I looked. I felt the tiny jerking movements as my eyes passed from one man to the other. The men shrank from my gaze.

"Yes, that's it, pretty Keturah. Look, look," Soor Lily whispered. "Wouldn't you be the perfect one to whom I could teach my magic arts? Aren't you the very daughter I should have had? And don't I keep smelling plague in the air? What if the road is not enough? If only you could love one of my sons, perhaps one of them might live . . ."

I studied the face of each one, and still the charm, bless-edly, looked and looked and did not cease in its looking. At last I said, utterly relieved, "I have looked, and I will not love any of them, Soor Lily."

Soor Lily put her long white hand on her bosom and made a sound like a wounded bird. "Not even one?" she whimpered.

"Not even a little," I said.

She looked at them sorrowfully. "It is hard to believe, but it must be true," she said. "Run and play now, sons."

They vanished so quickly and silently that it was as if they had never been there.

"Goodbye," she said to me.

"Not yet, Soor Lily. I have somewhat to say to you."

She cowered a little. "Of course," she said meekly.

"You are no wise woman," I said.

She shook her head regretfully. "Not wise, not wise at all," she murmured.

"I paid your price, didn't I?" Panic rose in my voice. "Did I not pay? Did I not save your son alive?"

"Yes, yes! He is whole again, my baby," she said. Her shoulders rounded and her head hung.

"But your love charm is not working. It slows down for Ben, but it does not stop. You tricked me," I said with all the indignation I could muster.

With the other half of my anger, I took the eye out of my pocket and placed it on the table. She gazed at it, appalled, as if it were a severed hand.

In desperation, I spoke my heart. "Oh, woman, what shall

I do?" I pleaded. "Perhaps it was the wrong eye, and it is the other eye that is necessary. You do have powers, don't you?"

As if it caused her the greatest distress to say so, she said, "Yes. Oh, lass, that I do."

I clutched her arm, which was as hard as a man's. "I must marry today—don't you see? I must marry my true love today . . . or—or go to *him*."

She nodded. "Yes," she said. "Yes, I thought as much." Slowly she placed a long, pale finger on the eye. "There could be only one reason why it keeps looking," she said sadly. "Only one reason."

"Yes," I declared. "You bungled the ingredients. You cheated me."

"Bungled, cheated," she repeated, as if she were considering the possibility. Then she shook her head slowly. "No. No bungling nor no cheating, lass," she said. "Only one reason."

"What, then?" I begged. "Tell me, what is the reason?"

"Keturah, you already love another. It looks for the true love you already have."

I opened my mouth to laugh or rage, I did not know which—but no sound came. She looked into my open mouth curiously, as if she could read in my throat the words that would not come.

Finally I said, "No. I do not love another. That is the problem, Soor Lily."

"Yes," she said gently, calmly. "You already love. True love. So sorry. A tragedy."

"Why should I lie to you? I do not love!"

"True love." She began to blubber. "So sad, so sad . . ."

"Stop it!" I insisted.

Immediately she stopped. Her sad face vanished and she beamed at me, happy to be pleasing me. She placed the eye gingerly back into my apron pocket and took me by the arm. "Goodbye, sweetums," she said, guiding me toward the door. "Goodbye, good luck, God bless," she murmured, as she pressed me out the door. "So pretty . . . Goodbye."

I stumbled back to the road, half-blind with fear and confusion and anger.

Already love!

I stood upon the cobbled road, unsure what to do, where to go.

No, I finally determined. I would go back. I had seen Soor Lily's handiwork, and I knew it had great power. She must try again.

I turned to go back to her house, but just off the road stood one of her great sons.

"Goodbye," he said.

I thought to walk around him, but I saw that all seven of her sons were guarding the way.

"Goodbye," another said. "Goodbye," said each in turn.

I walked back to Tide-by-Rood and to home.

# X

Of Tailor and Choirmaster and what I decide;
of good lemons and bad news.

Gretta and Beatrice had let themselves in and had done all
my chores. Now they were stitching, and their faces were
filled with worry. Grandmother was sleeping still.

"I have been to see Soor Lily," I said quietly, and I began
steeping foxglove tea.

"The charm is not working, is it?" Gretta said flatly.

"She says it is because I am in love already."

"It must be Ben."

"It must be, but the eye does not stop for Ben—it only
slows."

"It is waiting for your pie," Beatrice said hopefully.

"Perhaps," I said. I sat on the edge of Grandmother's
bed with the foxglove tea and stroked her hair until she
woke with a smile.

While I helped her sip the tea, Gretta and Beatrice
whispered together. Before Grandmother had finished the
tea, the color had come back to her face and I had persuaded her to have breakfast.

"You were right, Keturah," she said. "Death is not as
near as I had thought, perhaps."

After she had eaten, she took up her spindle and assured

me that she might feel well enough to make supper also.

"If you are well enough, Grandmother Reeve," Gretta said, "might we borrow Keturah for a time?"

"Of course, dears, run and play. Ah, youth is so carefree and innocent."

My friends escorted me outside and pounced upon me immediately. "You have not looked at every man while you held the charm," Gretta said accusingly. "Have you?"

"Indeed I have," I said. "At the hunt, at the gatherings, among the work crew . . ."

"Tailor?" Gretta demanded.

"Tailor—no . . ."

"Choirmaster?" Beatrice asked.

"Choirmaster—no . . ."

"Just as we thought," Gretta said, her hands on her hips.

"But they are for you!" I said. "Gretta, confess that you love Tailor yourself."

"It is true that I admire him, Keturah. He is kind to his children, and he mends Hermit Gregor's trousers for free. But a man who does good of his own free will is a man who cannot be bossed—and that, Keturah, can be a dangerous thing. Besides, I saw dirt in the corners of his house."

"Not everyone, perhaps, can be as perfect as you, Gretta," I said.

"Sister, friend," she said sternly to me, "we show ourselves in everything we do. Dirty floors, dirty soul; unmade bed, unkempt soul. Perfection in cleanliness demonstrates perfection of being. Every perfect stitch is a glory to God. Now that man, he lives in—"

"Comfort," I said.

"Sloth," said Gretta. "His garden has nine weeds. I counted them myself."

"Then it must please you that he demands perfection in stitches," I said.

"See the way his poor children are forced to dress—in rags and patches," she continued.

"I have seen them," I said. "They are no worse off than the poor shepherds down the way."

"Master Tailor is not poor," Gretta snapped.

"He is thrifty, perhaps," I said.

"He has such dear children. Perfect, in fact. But he and his orange hose!" Then she said, lost in reverie, "So hairy and muscled is he, he seems more suited to smithing than sewing."

Beatrice said to me, "And if the eye cannot bear to gaze upon Tailor's orange hose, surely it will cease to look when you hear the music Choirmaster has written for the king."

"Beatrice, you know you love him yourself!" I declared.

"I shall have no husband but shall go to heaven pure," she said with a grand turn of her head.

"And what, my friend, can be more purifying than to give your whole self and heart to another?" I countered. "Of course I could never love Choirmaster, nor Tailor."

"Did not Soor Lily say that you already loved?"

"She did, but . . ."

"Then you must try everyone. Come!" Gretta insisted. And they locked their arms in mine and walked me down to Tailor's cottage. I confess I was too tired to argue with them, let alone tear myself away. I even leaned upon them as I walked, so weary was I.

Tailor was gracious when we arrived at his door. It was a solid, simple home, well-built and warm, but plain. The furniture was made to withstand the use and abuse of children, and the whole room smelled of an abundance of good things to eat. There was not a flower or a curtain to be seen, but it was a house full of enough.

"Come in, Keturah, Gretta, Beatrice," he said, gesturing for us to enter his comfortable home. Gretta looked at me hopefully and nodded to my apron.

"Thank you, Keturah," Tailor said, "for helping with Lady Temsland's gown."

"Gown?"

Gretta laid some stitchery on the solid table. "The gown you have been working on, Keturah," she said encouragingly. Then to Tailor she said, "She wishes that you would wait no longer to see her stitches."

"Of course," said Tailor. He picked up the gown and turned it so that he could see the seams Gretta had sewn on the skirt. At first his look was stern, as if he were summoning the strength to tell me to begin again. But as he examined the stitches, looking more and more closely, his expression softened and then became one of admiration.

"This is very good work, Keturah," he said at last.

I blushed to hear him praise me for work I had not done, but he took my blushes for modesty.

"You need not be shy about these seams, Keturah," he said. "I see only five stitches that are not perfection."

"Five!" burst out Gretta.

He nodded to her briefly, then turned his eyes upon me again as if he were wondering how my art had escaped his notice so far.

"Five bad stitches? Where? You must be mistaken," Gretta spluttered.

"Here," he said. "And here, and these two, and this one."

Gretta and I both peered at the stitches he pointed out. Then she straightened and said very stiffly, "They are not as exact as the others."

"Why, sir," I said, "the hand that sewed these stitches has not made five wrong ones since it was as many years old," I said.

"But he is right, Keturah," Gretta said with injured pride. "They are not perfect." She looked meaningfully at my apron pocket where the charm lay.

Gretta looked so fierce that I touched the charm in my pocket. Yes—yes, I admired him, but . . . no, I did not love him. The eye twitched and quivered as rapidly as ever.

I shook my head slightly at Gretta. She sighed and then regarded Tailor as if it were all his fault. "Master Tailor, you have beautiful children. But why, Master Tailor," Gretta asked, "do your children run in rags when all the other children have new clothes?"

"They shall have new clothes when they learn to sew them themselves," he said. "I will teach them, but I will not sew for them."

Gretta scowled at him, but he seemed not to notice. "So you will only let them wear clothes given to them by other people?" she asked brusquely.

"Just so," Tailor said.

The eye flickered wildly in my hand until I could not stand to hold it anymore, and I took my hand out of my apron pocket. Behind us, Beatrice sighed.

"Good day, Tailor," Gretta said.

"Good day, Gretta," Tailor said mildly. "And thank you again, Keturah."

"Insufferable man," Gretta murmured as we walked out. "To let his children dress so. Of course you could not fall in love with such a man, Keturah."

"Gretta, it is not his fault that I cannot love him."

"It is just as well," she said. "I do not think I could bear to look at his orange hose when I came to visit you."

"Come, then," Beatrice said. "We are to church."

"No, no, I am so tired," I complained.

"Then the sooner you take a good look at Choirmaster with the charm, the sooner you can go home to rest," she said. I was so unused to Beatrice being firm that I resisted no more.

***

We entered the little chapel. Choirmaster was bent over his music, making notes. When he looked up, his sad expression softened a bit.

"Keturah!" he said, glad to see me. He was almost smiling—I scarcely recognized him with that hint of a smile. "Your cousin Bill is everything you promised. Thank you for sending him to me. Our choir will be fit for a king after all."

Beatrice, turning pink, made a small gesture toward my apron pocket while Choirmaster extolled the virtues of my cousin's voice and noted, becoming sad again, how remarkable it was that, though in the same family, I had not been given the smallest portion of this gift.

All this he said while I steeled myself and reached into my apron pocket. The eye was looking so fast and hard that it nearly jumped out of my grasp.

I shook my head a little at Beatrice, and she turned a sour eye to Choirmaster, as if he had failed her in the gravest of ways.

"Choirmaster," she said, "Bill tells me that he believes he knows the reason you are so sad all the time. It is because you are lonely. It is because you are in want of a wife."

I gasped a little, surprised that my timid friend would speak so boldly, and Gretta hid a smile.

"So he is as perceptive as he is talented," Choirmaster replied. "He has guessed my secret. I am lonely indeed, but there must be no marriage for me."

"But why?" Beatrice asked.

"If I waste my love on women there will be none left for music. Mother taught me that."

"But you are a grown man," she said.

"I hear her voice," Choirmaster said, "even over the music. I hear it. Remember, son, she would say. Remember that music alone will get you to heaven."

His eyes searched the empty air above him, perhaps looking for her ghost. He rubbed his knuckles as if they smarted. "She taught me every day to give up the things of the world. All of it was wickedness, she told me. Music, she said, was the language of heaven. I must give myself to music."

"Is she nearby, Choirmaster? I thought you came from a far distance."

"Oh, yes, she is nearby, though not in a place you can reach by foot or by carriage. But she is nearby. I can feel it. She would whip my fingers, Mother would, every time I made a mistake in my music. It was a dainty golden whip she used. I feel it, I feel it every time I wish to love another."

Beatrice said gently, "Come, it cannot be so bad."

"My mother wanted to be God's bride, but her father would not have it. He feared what God would do to him when He discovered what kind of a wife he'd raised his daughter to be. So he married my mother to an organ builder who drank too much. She raised me on music. Before I could say 'Mama,' I could play a sonata. Every waking moment I practiced. I gave her little whip the name Tooth, for it bit."

"For this I am sorry," I said. Beatrice made small sympathy sounds, and Gretta covered her mouth.

"Are *you* sorry, Beatrice?" Choirmaster asked with much feeling.

"Choirmaster, your music reminds me of every sad thought I ever had," she said. "Your music would wrench the heart of the devil himself. Perhaps if you made your music . . . happier, you would hear your mother's voice less, and someone could comfort your heart."

"There can be no comfort for me but from my music,"

he said dolefully. And he sat down at the organ to play so sad a tune that I had to hurry away.

Gretta and Beatrice soon caught up with me.

"Well, you tried," Gretta said.

"It must be Ben," I said. "The eye only waits to see if I can make a pie tasty enough to win Best Cook. I'm sure of it."

Beatrice patted my arm. "Rest. Later we will think about pies."

I shook my head, and though my whole body was weary, I did not slow my pace.

"There is no time. Tomorrow is the fair, and if there is any possibility I will live to see it, today I must make pies."

---

Grandmother was in the garden when we arrived home, and looking so well that it cheered my heart and gave me renewed strength. I started on squash pie.

Just as I was finishing, someone knocked at the door. Gretta rose to answer it. When she opened the door, there stood Ben Marshall with another baby-sized squash in his arms. With a wooden spoon in one hand and a whisk in the other, I beamed at him. Behind him was Padmoh, and in her arms were several bunches of lettuce.

"Come in, Ben," Grandmother said, "and you, Padmoh. We are just about to feast upon a pie Keturah made from your delicious squash, Ben. Sit, sit, both of you. How fortunate we are that you grow such big squashes, Ben, for then you have much to share."

"I've brought another. Keturah, you are dusted all over

with flour. You look so . . . pretty."

Oh, handsome Ben, I thought. Good, solid Ben—but would I always have to be covered in flour and sugar to be beautiful to him? It made me more tired to think of it. Still, he was very handsome.

"I thought what a generous thing it was of Ben to bring squashes to the poor," Padmoh said, "so I offered to carry lettuces. And besides, Mother Marshall bade me come."

Ben looked at her as if she were a stray cat that had followed him home. Grandmother served them portions of the pie I had made, and Ben set right to eating.

"I am practicing for the cooking contest tomorrow," I said, dearly wishing there would be a tomorrow.

Padmoh sat down, too, and gingerly took a taste.

"It's delicious," Ben said after a mouthful.

"There is a certain aftertaste," Padmoh said delicately, "but it is quite good."

Grandmother turned the talk to the beautification of the village, and Ben and even Padmoh and my friends talked about the wonders of it.

"Mistress Smith and some other women went to Hermit Gregor's house," Ben said. "They scrubbed and tossed and folded and washed and swept and gardened until he wept and promised to be a better man."

Everyone laughed.

Padmoh said genteelly, "Widow Harker, who beds her cow in her house for want of a shed, came home today to find a sweet, clean shed for her cow."

Ben noticed I was quiet and said, "With pie like this,

Keturah, you could win Best Cook at fair time."

"I am glad you like it," I said.

Padmoh scowled at him and then at me. "It is hard to tell such a thing from pies," she said. "Besides, didn't he say that very thing to me the other day. Fickle Ben."

"But I do believe this pie makes Keturah a fraction better," Ben said.

Gretta and Beatrice smiled, and Padmoh stabbed violently at the pie with her fork. I felt sorry that she was unhappy, but I was relieved that Ben had loosened his tongue in favor of my chances.

Just then there was a weak knock at the door, and I opened it to see Tobias standing with lemons in his hands.

I threw my arms around him, then took the lemons. "Why, they are beautiful, Tobias! So plump, so fresh. Did they cost very much?"

Slowly he held out the second set of coins John Temsland had given him. "Not a penny, Keturah, and yet they were very dear."

Only then did I notice that he was most pale, whiter than the gray dust around his mouth and eyes.

"How did you get them, then?"

"It is a strange tale I have to tell, Keturah."

"Sit, and tell it," I said. He sat down slowly, feeling for the chair as if he were blind. Gretta put her hand on her brother's shoulder.

"I looked and looked, Keturah," he began. "No one had lemons. At last I thought to go to the road that heads to Great Town, only to the crossroads, in hopes of seeing a merchant who might tell me where to find them. And sure enough, Keturah, I met there a man who had many wondrous wares in his cart. I told him my errand, that the best cook of Tide-by-Rood needed lemons. Lemons, says he, why I have lemons here, all the way from Spain. I would have them, sir, I said. But when I held out the coins Lord Temsland gave me, he shook his head. Not enough, said he. Take it, sir, I said, and tell what I can do to make up the difference. Whatever it is, I said, I will do it. He snatched the coins, and said that if I would serve him for one round year, I should have paid the price in full.

"But I need the lemons now, for Keturah Reeve must cook a dish for the king, I said. Very well, said he, then I must get a year's work out of you in a single month. No, sir, I said, the lemons must be delivered now. Then you have no bargain, said he. Give me back my coins, I said. No, I shall not—good day, he said.

"Mistress Keturah, you know I am not good at wrestling, but I knew you and the young lord and the queen must have lemons. So I tackled him. He was a tall man, and much fatter than me, but it was for the lemons, you see. He beat me soundly, and then picked up his donkey prod with which to finish the fight. I thought I was going to lose my life, as well as the coins, for which I was most sorry on account of your needing lemons.

"The merchant raised the prod, and as he was about to bring it down upon my head, he stopped cold and stared into nothingness. Pale he went, gray as the underbelly of a fish. He shook his head once, and nodded once, as if he were having a conversation with a ghost. I shivered in fear to see his countenance, so full of terror it was. The prod dropped, forgotten.

"At last he turned his eyes to me. Blank with horror, they were, but utterly resigned. Death has come for me, he said. I have cheated him many times, and now he comes to collect his debt. He gives me one last chance, before I go with him, to atone for the suffering I have brought to others through my cheating ways. Lad, the merchant says to me, there are coins sewn into my coat. They are all yours if you will forgive me.

"May I have the lemons, sir? asks I. He nodded once. Then I forgive you, I said. And he crumpled and dropped dead.

"His eyes were still open in death, and they seemed to look at me with gratitude. I waited beside him a long time, until it rained into his open eyes and the mule bawled for hunger. And I came home."

Tobias stared at the table, his lips parted as if he had not the strength to clamp his jaws together.

I raised the lemons to my nose. Did they not smell of the sun? My pie would bring sunshine and cloud to the palate. My pie would win Best Cook at the fair. My pie would win me Ben Marshall—

Tobias began to weep. "Keturah—he died of the plague."

# XI

*I bestow my first kiss.*

My lemons had brought plague. I had brought plague to my beloved Tide-by-Rood. Had Lord Death not warned us about Great Town? *Plague.* The word stopped up my ears and filled my mouth and throat so sufficatingly I could not speak for a moment.

Tobias put his face in his hands. "I am sick, Keturah," he said.

Gretta threw her arms around him, and I stroked his hair. "Do not be afraid," I said.

Tobias raised his face to me. His tears had mixed with the dust from the journey, making gray, chalky lines down his cheeks.

"You must tell no one what you know, and I will go to Lord Death," I said, and now I was crying too.

"It is too late to keep it secret," Gretta said. "Padmoh has already flown to spread the news."

"What are you going to do, Keturah?" Ben said to me, and there was fear and accusation in his voice. "Is it true that you have brought death into our midst?"

Down in the village I could hear shouts and screams.

"They will think you have brought the plague, Keturah," Beatrice said, her hands clasped as if in prayer.

"But I have, my friend," I said. "They will be right."

Gretta went to the window. "They are coming!" she said.

Grandmother came to me in her nightdress. "You must go into the wood and hide, Keturah," she said, and her voice was chillingly calm. "I will pretend you are here and not let them in. I will forestall them as long as I can."

"I will go into the forest, though not to hide," I said.

Just then I heard a clattering of hooves on the cobbles outside, and a great pounding at the door.

"Ben, you must protect Grandmother," I said.

"I? How can I protect her from a mob?" said Ben helplessly.

Again there was pounding, and the door flew open. In the doorway stood John Temsland and Henry and a number of young men.

"We will disperse the mob," John said. He dismounted. "Take my horse and flee, Keturah. Run away. Go to my father at the king's court. I will find you there."

"No, I go to the forest. Protect Grandmother. Be silent about where I am, and trust me."

I took Tobias's hand and ran out the back door and into the forest. We ran together until we could no longer hear the cries of the villagers. "Now we must wait," I said. "He will come. He always comes."

And truly it was not long before Lord Death on his horse emerged from the trees, his cloak billowing behind him like great black wings. He rode slowly and surely. His face was beautiful and terrible with resolve.

In the light of day he seemed appalling. How dare he ride in the sunlight without apology, without shame? He and his great horse were together a massive shadow that drained the light out of the day. The horse's feet drew down the clouds in their wake, so that it seemed he walked in fog. The trees greedily sucked up the sunlight and left none but deep green shadows to drift down to the forest floor.

"Oh, Lord of Heaven," Tobias whispered beside me. "I can see him now, too."

The freckles on his face stood out in bold relief. There was no time to comfort him.

Lord Death looked down at me from a great height, and his expression was dark with bitter power. The clouds that now covered the sun made the whole world gray, and even the leaves seemed of doubtful color. Tobias crossed himself and began to rock.

Lord Death dismounted and bowed to me, a stately bow, and I returned it with the deepest of curtseys. He did not flinch from my gaze, nor I from his. My eyes asked him, asked him why, why, why.

At last he said, "It would have been enough, the changes you have made in the village, but—"

"It's my fault—my lemons. I brought the plague," I said.

"I warned you to stay away from Great Town," he said, turning a withering look upon Tobias. Tobias whimpered. A wind arose. Black clouds banked higher and higher upon one another, as if the whole earth were burning and the sky were choking with dark smoke.

"Why?" I asked. "Why would you destroy our people, the innocents?"

"Are they so innocent, Keturah?" he asked. "Those who gather against you and would burn you alive even now if they could find you?" His voice made the ground beneath me shake.

"Do you think I don't know that the plague does not pick and choose? What of the children, the little children? What of them?" I asked. My voice sounded small and lost, as if drowned in a great wind. But he heard me.

"If untimely death came only to those who deserved that fate, Keturah, where would choice be? No one would do good for its own sake, but only to avoid an early demise. No one would speak out against evil because of his own courageous soul, but only to live another day. The right to choose is man's great gift, but one thing is not his to choose—the time and means of death."

To this I had no answer.

I knew what I must do.

I raised my palms to him. "Forgive me," I said. I did not recognize my own voice, it was so choked and piteous.

There was a crack of lightning in the distance, and again thunder, only closer now. The gray clouds above us began to roil and blacken, but there was no smell of rain. The air was dry as old bones.

"Do not ask, Keturah!" he commanded quietly, but in his voice was the hint of a plea.

"Forgive me, my lord," I said, "but I must ask."

"It is too late," he said. "Goody Thompson and her

husband and her two babies are already sick with it. And others . . . It is too late."

"No, sire, no. I know that nothing is too late for you. I ask—I ask—"

"Keturah!" His cry echoed against the clouds as if his voice and the thunder were one sound.

"My lord, I ask—"

"Do you dare, Keturah?" The sky around us was near as dark as night, and lightning snaked silently overhead. Tobias fell to his knees beside me, then fainted utterly away. The thunder and the wind roared around me.

"His life! His life and"—I raised my hands higher—"and all of Tide-by-Rood! And the king, and—and you must make my friends happy, though I die. I do ask. You cannot deny me!"

I did not look up. I saw his boots before me. And then, though the wind thrashed in the grass and rocked the forest, though the black sky railed and lightning flashed, all near us became silent. In the silence, his voice spoke into my heart.

"Keturah, don't you know your soul is mine? Not a man on this earth, no king, no wise man, is greater than I. Every one of them humbles himself before me one day. Yet you, Keturah, a peasant girl, bargain with me, rob me, and ask greater and greater favors of me—all the while saying you will marry for love! What do you say to this?"

The wind in my face made it hard to breathe. "What if, this time, I gave you something," I said. "Something precious."

Dark shadows leapt around him. "There is nothing you could give me," he said, with great dignity.

I stepped closer to him.

I traveled a hundred miles in that single step. In a stride, my village was so far away I could scarcely remember it. It would be a journey of a thousand days to return.

There was no breath in him, no flush of blood, no taint of sweat or tears. Next to him, I felt the grossness of my own body, how more I was like the earth than I was like him. He was air and wind and cloud and bird; I was dust and worm.

I was suddenly aware that he might not want what I could give him, but I had nothing else so precious.

Another step.

"Keturah," he said. I felt him lift his hand as if to touch my hair, and something in his eyes was warm, though he exuded cold.

And as his lips parted to speak again, I pressed my lips gently against his.

Had I truly thought I would not die when I kissed him? But I did. For a moment the breath and life went out of me, and there was no time and no tomorrow, but only my lips against his. I stepped away quickly, back into my life, panting for breath.

His lordly demeanor had vanished, and his countenance held nothing but astonishment and—and something else I could not name.

"I have kissed you," I said, breathless.

The shadows around his face lightened.

"Now—now you are at my command," I said triumphantly, trembling. "You must obey my every wish," I said, in a voice a little more subdued.

He shook his head slightly.

"But—but I have kissed you," I said, blushing and uncertain. "Please, it is not for me that I ask."

"Do not dare," he said sadly.

"So you must help me, Lord Death. Is one kiss not enough? Then here . . ."

I kissed him again.

"And here..."

This time I felt his arms reach round me, and he enfolded me to himself and kissed me in return. In the first moment, I could not believe he was death—he was a man, and no more. In the next, I was afraid and I pushed at him. It was futile—his strength was more than that of a hundred men. And so he kissed me until my blood ran so cold it burned.

He stopped suddenly, and stepped away so violently I almost fell. My lips were numb with cold, and my throat ached with cold, and my stomach was icy and empty.

"Here is danger!" he said sternly.

I raised my face to him. "Sir, I know you can do anything . . ." His eyes were not the clouded, vacant eyes of one dead. Instead they were clear—I thought I could see the endless night sky in his eyes, and the stars too. Unspeakable sorrow was there, and matchless beauty.

"And why can I not deny you, Keturah?" His voice was insistent. I could not answer but with the truth.

"Because you love me!"

The silence into which we spoke vanished, and the wind roared in my ears again.

"It is true," he said, his voice both quiet and piercing.

A deafening crack of lightning, a roll of thunder so loud I felt it in my throat, and rain began to pour out of the sky.

"Your beloved village is safe," Lord Death said, and I heard his voice clearly over the storm. "You have until the end of the fair, and then I will send the hart for you."

I wondered if he had spoken not aloud but into the airless places of my secret mind.

The rain woke Tobias. He stared at me with eyes too wide open and did not move and did not look about.

Lord Death mounted his horse and in the next moment was gone, and I knelt beside Tobias.

"Is he . . . ?" Tobias asked.

"He is gone." I stroked his hair. "The plague is taken from us."

He lay crying for a little time, and I could not tell the rain from the tears on his face. Then, slowly, he sat up. The rain had already begun to spend itself, and the sun began to glint through the clouds.

He stood, testing each limb as if sensing the life within. He swayed on his feet a moment and then smiled. "I will live," he whispered. "I feel it, I feel it sure. You did it, Keturah!" he said. "I owe you my life."

I put my hand over his mouth.

"Not I, Tobias. Not I. Lord Death gave it to you, as he

does every day. Never forget this."

"But . . ."

"Never forget."

Tobias smiled. "All I know is, I am alive, and I feel well, Keturah. There is no sickness in me at all."

"Come," I said, "let us go see to the others."

# XII

⬦

*Many startling confessions,*
*and I am saved from a terrible fate.*

When Tobias and I emerged from the forest, we were not where I thought we would be. We were south of the village, at the place where the cart path turned into our newly cobbled road.

Tobias and I took our way silently into the village. It was strangely quiet and still, and my heart smote me a moment, fearful that Lord Death had lied to me.

But there walked Tobias beside me, strong and whole and ruddy, and even if he had not been with me, as evidence, I knew I need not doubt Lord Death's word. My village was saved.

And yet those words did not echo in my heart as I had once thought they would. I had made friends with death, and it would no longer hold fears for me.

Thomas Red was walking alone with his mule. He saw me and Tobias, and bowed as if I were a titled lady.

"Keturah Reeve," he said. "Well met. Would you do me the honor of riding my mule into town, where the villagers gather? It would be my very great honor, for I have heard and seen that you have saved us from the plague."

"Not I," I said, "but one I know."

"But he would not have saved us without you," Tobias said.

I had not the strength to contradict both of them, and a ride seemed a good thing just then. And so I rode upon the mule, along our beautiful cobbled road, and soon we saw the villagers in a throng ahead of us. When they saw us, they parted and stood on either side of the road. They fell silent as we approached.

A child threw a handful of posies onto the road before me, and others began to whisper my name. Soon there was laughter, and someone cheered, and then they all cheered. I looked about me in wonder until we came to the square.

At the high end stood John Temsland. Tobias led me to him, and I dismounted from the mule and curtseyed.

The villagers gathered in a circle around us. Goody Thompson and her husband were closest to me.

"Forgive us," Goody said, while her man twisted his cap and looked at the ground. I smiled to see them healthy and whole with their beautiful boys.

I glanced round at the crowd, whose faces seemed suddenly unfamiliar. The air of the village shimmered with an angle of light I did not recognize. I searched for Gretta and Beatrice, and when I found them they smiled and nodded encouragingly.

"I would reward you, Keturah. What favor might I grant you?" John said quietly. "Ask anything. If it is in my power to give it, I will."

In that moment I wished for nothing more than to be the girl I had once been—a girl with hopes of love and a peasant baby of her own to hold, a girl with her whole life clear before her. I wished only for everything to be as it had been before I followed the hart into the forest, before I knew the shadow that the forest could cast in my heart.

"Sire, if you would do ought for me," I said, "I would wish it to be this: that you speak no more of it—that we forget past sorrows and ready ourselves for the fair and for the king's visit."

John Temsland studied me for a long moment, then said, "So be it. The king comes tomorrow, but tonight, when all is ready for the fair, there will be dancing." He looked around at the crowd. "Go. Ready yourselves."

And so the villagers filed away, the men nodding and the women dropping small curtseys to me as they went. Gretta and Beatrice made their way over to me, and we watched as people set up their booths. Some of the men erected a stand over the common for the king and his entourage and for Lord Temsland and his wife so they might watch the races and games and dramas that had been planned for entertainment. Atop the hill, silk banners in bright blue and yellow and orange were unfurled from the second floor of the manor house. Musicians began to set up their little bands, and everyone sang and laughed and talked. Women laid aside their spinning and weaving and brought their breads and buns and cakes and cookies, all covered in new, clean cloths. They brought their sewing and crafts and molded butter and soaps and round cheeses. Young men led their best calves and sheep and pigs to the showing pens, and old men tagged them and studied them with a serious eye. And everyone nodded in my direction and smiled.

Soon people forgot me in their haste to ready for the fair—all but Gretta and Beatrice.

"We don't know what stories to believe," Gretta said.

"Someday I will tell you the story as it really is, not how others will tell it, my friends," I said.

"When you wish," said Gretta.

"If you wish," said Beatrice.

I did not have the heart to tell them of my bond with Death. Besides, there was yet hope—did I not have lemons at home?

"Now I must go home and make my lemons into pie. But before I do, we have some errands to do, we three. Come." I led them to Tailor's house.

"But I have already delivered the gown, in your name, Keturah," Gretta said when she perceived where we were going.

"Just so," I said, and continued on. As we approached Tailor's home, his children came to greet us, but it was only Gretta they crowded around.

Tailor came out and welcomed us into his home. The children all followed. I stared in awe at the beautiful gown that hung ready for Lady Temsland. Tailor followed my gaze.

"It is fine work, Keturah," he said. "You have many surprising gifts."

"Sir, I have something to confess, and this is the reason for our visit," I said. "The gown is not my handiwork but Gretta's. The explanation of our deception is too long and complicated to give, but please accept my apologies. It is Gretta's fine work."

"Keturah!" Gretta exclaimed. "That is not true."

"Ah," Tailor said. Then he smiled. "Of course I knew, Gretta. Did you think that I could not recognize your fine seams?"

Gretta spluttered and blushed. "Keturah did it . . ."

Tailor continued, "No one else could do such work. In this whole piece there are not more than three faulty stitches."

Gretta's blush turned to paleness. "Three?" Her eyes narrowed. "Three? First five faulty stitches, and even now three! Come, children," she said huffily. "Let's go play." And she led them into the yard.

"She is a fine woman, but a proud one," Tailor said to the open door. "She told me not to wear orange." He smiled.

"Tailor," I said, "perhaps if you will humor her in the small things, you will hold sway in the bigger things. I know she would like to learn from you."

"Keturah, you have become wise," he said.

"Keturah!" Gretta called from the yard.

I bade him good day and went into the yard to see Gretta and to endure her chastisements.

"What of our plan, Keturah?" she asked angrily. "Why did you tell him?"

"Because, Gretta, I told you—he is not my one true love."

"Of course you don't love him. Who could love a man who wears orange hose? I told him about the weeds in his garden, and today I see they are still there, and bigger, too." She sighed. "He is an insufferable man," she said. "But you must forgive him, and then I am sure you will love him."

"Gretta," I said, "I have observed that you treat a man as an old garment to be taken apart and stitched again. Perhaps you could think of him as good cloth, rich fabric that wants only to be embroidered upon. And perhaps, if you will do that, you will see that you love Tailor yourself."

"What? I? Love Tailor?" She laughed aloud and then turned toward the door where Tailor still stood, gazing at her. She swallowed her laughter and returned his gaze.

Jane, the oldest of Tailor's children, said, "Do you, Gretta? If it is true, we would like to ask for your hand in marriage."

"What?"

"Papa says the clothes you secretly made us must be saved for his wedding day, and so we ask you if you can't please hurry up and marry him."

"You have made clothes for the children, Gretta?" I asked.

"Well, I couldn't let them run about in rags when all the other children had new clothes, could I?" she said.

The littlest one tugged on Gretta's skirt. "But will you marry us?"

She gathered them into her arms. "I love you dearly, but it is God's own truth that I don't love your papa."

The ragged children looked at one another in calm surprise. The eldest girl spoke up. "Papa says you do."

"He—he said that?" Gretta asked.

"Yes," said the lad. "But before Mama died, she made him promise that he would never remarry unless he found somebody who loved us even more than him. And then all of us had a dream last night. Mama came to us. Death allowed her to, she said. And she told us that Papa would never ask you on his own, and so we must ask you to marry us."

Gretta put her hands on either side of her face.

"Yes. And Papa believed us, and said we must do as our mama said," the boy continued.

The youngest one unplugged her thumb. "Papa said making clothes is nothing. He said if you had to care for us day and night, soon you wouldn't like us at all. Is that true, Gretta?"

She shook her head slowly at first, and then firmly. "Of course it is not true. If I cared for you a year and a day I would only love you more. It is your papa I would love less."

"So you do love him!" Jane said.

"No!"

"But you just said . . ."

"I . . ." Gretta spoke with great uncertainty. "I do not love your papa, Jane. I love you, but not him. Not at all. No, no. And I never have. And I never will. And I never could. Impossible."

The children looked at one another again. "Poor Papa," the lad said at last.

They examined their dirty feet closely. "Yes, poor Papa," said the youngest.

"Poor? But why?" Gretta asked, touching their sad faces.

"Because he loves *you*."

"He—" Gretta took her apron hem and dabbed at her temples. "He what?"

"Papa loves you with a dying and infernal love," the youngest girl said.

"Undying," the eldest corrected. "And eternal."

Tailor, who could hear all, stood quietly in the doorway still, his eyes only upon Gretta and a small smile on his face.

"That cannot be," Gretta said. She had flushed into a flaming red.

"We know," the eldest girl said. "We have known him all our lives."

I could not exactly read Gretta's face. It might have been disbelief there in her eyes, or perhaps an inordinate surprise in the lines of her forehead. It might have been the countenance of one who had seen an angel on the way. She deliberately avoided looking at Tailor.

I kissed Gretta on the cheek. "I am so happy," I said.

Gretta pulled me into her embrace, then let me go.

"Come, Beatrice," I said. "I have an errand with you." I took her arm and led her away, down toward the church. Once I glanced back to see Tailor bow Gretta into his home, the children following as chaperones.

As we walked I thought upon the dream that all of Tailor's children had had. Surely Lord Death had arranged their mother's visitation. Could it be he had done it for me—because he knew I loved Gretta?

I was still marveling over these events when we arrived at the church. Choirmaster seemed to be waiting for us.

But it was soon clear that it was Bill he was awaiting, and impatiently, too.

"Where is he? Where is your cousin, Keturah? Today is the last day to practice!"

"Sir, I have somewhat to say to you concerning Bill, but it can only be said in privacy. Surely the other boys wish to go watch the preparations for the fair."

"Keturah—no!" Beatrice said.

After hesitating a moment, Choirmaster said, "I fear only a little what you could say, for I am happy today—not only for the tale I heard of you, Keturah, but in a personal matter as well. Singers, you are dismissed. But rest your voices!" They scattered like a flock of gulls, and soon we three were alone in the church.

"Choirmaster," I began, "it is not her fault—it was my idea—but we have a confession to make."

Beatrice held up her hand to stop me. "No, Keturah, you shall not take the blame for this. Haven't I longed every day of my remembered life to sing in his choir?" She turned to Choirmaster. "Sir," she said, "I am your Bill. I have been coming in disguise."

"Surely not!" he said with great surprise.

"But it is true," she replied.

"I cannot believe it!" he said.

And so Beatrice opened her mouth, and from it came music—oh, music that could break the heart of a dead man. When she stopped, Choirmaster said nothing for a long moment.

"Did you think I didn't know?" he said at last. "Would

I not recognize the voice I have loved since the first time I heard you sing in the congregation?"

Beatrice opened her mouth as if she would sing again, but no sound came out. Choirmaster smiled so broadly he was almost handsome. Then he became somber again. "But you must say not a word, or my choir—my choir would be nothing without you."

He took her hand and slowly, gently, folded it in his own as if it were a small bird.

"I've had the strangest dream, Beatrice," he said.

"Tell it to me, Choirmaster," Beatrice said in a softer voice. Neither of them seemed to remember that I was there.

"First I must explain something. I thought, after my mother died, that I would abandon my music. But I did not. No, I loved it all the more, and I did not abandon it. Because of him—Death. Because I saw him come for her, and I saw that, after all, she was just a girl, weak and mortal. When I glimpsed—only glimpsed, mind you—his black cape, I saw that all her life she'd sought strength against the day when he must come, and that only then did she realize that there is no strength on that day. Submission is all there is. So I played . . . to submit my heart every day so that it would not be the struggle it was for her." He sighed. "Now I will tell you the dream."

He paused for a moment and then began, "The one who came for her—he appeared to me last night. A tall man, dressed in black, at my bedside, great and terrible. Choirmaster, he said, I am Lord Death. Your mother would speak with you."

Beatrice put her other hand to her mouth.

"When he called her name, her spirit came scurrying, as if she had been called away from some pressing task. In her hand was her little gold whip.

"I hid my head beneath my quilt, but the tall man pulled the quilt away from me. Choirmaster, he said, it is time to be a man.

"I looked, and there was my mother standing at my bedside, holding the whip in her two hands as if she were offering it to me. I have come to ask your forgiveness, she said. She placed the whip on the bed beside me, and as she did she sighed. My torments are over, she said. Remember, son, that as much as music is a task of heaven, so is love. Be happy. She hurried away then, and I woke up."

Beatrice said tenderly, "It was only a dream, Choirmaster."

"Perhaps," he said. Then he drew a little golden whip from his robe. "I buried this with her," he said, "but it was on my bed when I awoke."

After a moment he said, "Beatrice, come with me into the chapel. I would speak to you alone."

I left them and returned home, smiling to myself.

I picked up the lemons that were still on the table, almost forgotten. I cut one and tasted it. It was so sour it brought tears to my eyes.

"Grandmother," I said, "do you suppose that with a bitter fruit such as this I might make a pie?"

"Of course," she said, "if you sweeten it with sugar. Here,

use it all, my Keturah, for I feel in my bones that after today we shall never have to worry about sugar again."

And so I cooked, while Grandmother went to see who would be showing what at the fair and to receive congratulations for having such a clever granddaughter.

*

I cooked and tasted and cooked more and tasted more, and at last I had a filling that was not too sweet and not too tart. That was for the sun. For the topping, I whipped egg whites and sugar until they fluffed like summer-day clouds, and then I baked.

Finally I had a pie that I knew would make every man in the village fond of me, and make Ben Marshall love me enough to propose.

While I cooked with a fury, a knock came at the door. It was Ben himself.

I smiled at him hopefully.

"Keturah," he said, "the fair is tomorrow."

"I am making a special pie, Ben," I said. "It is a lemon pie."

"May I?" He held out his hand for the spoon, which was coated in the glistening filling.

He tasted. His eyes grew larger. He licked the spoon again.

"Keturah, it is delicious!"

He licked the spoon until he had cleaned every drop of filling off it. "It is unlike anything I have tasted before. It is wonderful! Surely you will win Best Cook at the fair."

With that, he fell upon one knee. "Keturah, will you marry me?"

"Why, Ben, I—I don't yet have the ribbon."

"But you will. And if not, Father need only taste your pie to know that you should have won. Say you will marry me, Keturah."

My heart fluttered once, like a dying butterfly, and then was still. Utterly still and silent. "One moment," I said. I put my hand in my apron pocket and gripped the charm tightly. Yes, this was the man Soor Lily referred to when she said I was already in love. Surely he was.

No. The eye in the charm looked. Slowly it rolled in my hand, like a sad shaking of the head.

My heart was as mute as a stone within my bosom.

"No!" I said aloud to my heart.

Ben looked confused.

"I—I mean, no, I should win fairly, Ben," I stammered. "What if the crust is tough?"

He stood up. "Do not concern yourself, Keturah." And then he tried to kiss me.

I pushed him away. "Sir," I said, "I beg you."

Again he looked confused. "Very well. Of course I respect your maidenly modesty. We shall wait until your pie has won, fair and square, and I shall propose to you on the spot."

He grabbed my hand, kissed it, and left. I stood still, spoon in hand, and watched him walk away. I squeezed the charm as if I would cease its rolling. I did not bother to close the door.

"Stupid girl," I said to myself at last. I began scrubbing the kitchen, berating myself all the while. Did not every girl in Tide-by-Rood dream of this? But Ben was not my true love, and I needed no charm to tell me so.

I scrubbed so hard I almost knocked over the pie, and then in frustration I ran from the house. I ran and ran, searching, searching the eyes of every man I saw. Who was he, this man I wanted to love? It was not only to free myself from Death's bond that I searched. What good was my life if my heart would not love?

Soon I had followed all the village paths and looked at every man who smiled at me, and came at last to Hermit Gregor's. His cottage had been cleaned and whitewashed by the women of the village, but already he was beginning to make new piles: a pile of bones, a pile of hair and threads and sheep wool, a pile of rocks, and a pile of refuse from around the village. I could see his dirty, hairy face just inside the window.

"Come out, Hermit Gregor," I called sweetly.

"You aren't here to clean, are you?" he whimpered.

"No, Hermit. I am here to see if I love you."

I heard a terrified squeal, and his head disappeared. Boldly I entered his house. He was half-hidden beneath a pile of straw that served as his bed. I could see only the lower half of him, and it was trembling.

"Be a man, Hermit Gregor," I demanded, "and look at me."

"Why would you want to love me?" he cried from beneath the straw.

"So I might marry you, of course."

"Marry!" He wiggled farther under the straw.

"Look at me," I said, "or I shall call my friend Lord Death to visit you." Slowly he emerged from the straw and sullenly looked in my eyes. The eye rolled so hard it almost wrenched from my grasp.

I shuddered and ran thankfully away.

Evening had fallen and the lanterns had been lit and the music and the dancing begun when I returned slowly to the common. I hovered on the fringes of the crowd, hopeless, until Gretta and Beatrice found me and drew me into the thick of things. I was immediately asked to dance.

I tried to love every boy and bachelor who requested a dance, to no avail. A calmness had settled over me. Somewhere, as Soor Lily said, I already loved someone.

Everyone, married and unmarried, asked to dance with me, and all were kind and gracious. But it was hard to enjoy my honor when I was half in forever, and when the eye jittered and rolled in my hand for every man.

Grandmother and her old friends watched as I danced, and I saw her shine with pride for the gentle things they said of me. Sometimes the dancing stopped for acrobatics and singing, and there was even a play. It was a glorious night.

At the height of the festivities, I was asked to dance again, this time by John Temsland.

My friends, and indeed all the other villagers, stood agape as John led me onto the dance floor. Gradually, in an effort not to stare, some couples joined us in dancing, but

Gretta and Beatrice continued to stare at me and would not pay attention to anyone who asked for a dance.

John was wearing a tunic the color of pale straw and breeches the green of the forest. His hair was loose and long, his skin browned by the labor on the road, and his eyes were blue as the banners that hung from the manor.

"Sir," I said.

He twirled me, then drew me in a little closer. "I want to extend my personal thanks, Keturah," he said.

"That is unnecessary, sir," I said. "You do me honor enough with this dance."

"Please, Keturah, say my name."

"John," I said shyly, "do not thank me."

"I do not understand everything that happened today," John said, "but I saw with my own eyes the great swellings on Goody and the child. I saw him sicken, and then with my own eyes saw him heal as the rain came."

I said nothing, thinking of the rain and of Lord Death.

"Tales of this day will be told for generations," he said, "but I hope that sometime you will tell me the real story."

"Of course—John," I said. "But you must know that in me is no great courage, but only, perhaps, a great love for my people."

"As befits a lady," John said. He twirled me again and then stepped closer to me. "I asked my mother, Keturah," he said, very low, "how a lord's son might go about marrying a commoner."

"What commoner?" I asked, astonished.

"I know you think it is impossible. Even Mother is

doubtful. But listen—who is the one person with the power to turn a common woman into a lady? The king! His Majesty the king, the very king who is coming to Tide-by-Rood for the fair."

"John," I said, shaking my head, "the king does not raise up commoners except for war heroes or wealthy merchants."

"Remember, Keturah, remember what the king promised to the one who wins top prize at the fair?"

"His shoe full of gold and a wish granted."

"Yes. And I will win," he said.

"Truly? And with what will you win?" I asked, smiling at his confidence.

He gestured sweepingly. "Tide-by-Rood is what I will contribute to the fair, Keturah."

"Sir, it is a glorious contribution. But what common woman will receive this honor, if I may ask?"

"You, Keturah."

I stopped still and began to dance again only when I saw people staring.

"You helped me see what Tide-by-Rood could be," he said. "You inspired me, Keturah. For this you will be made a lady. *My* lady."

A lady!

Suddenly all weariness left me. I found myself swirling to the music.

A lady!

The villagers honored me, and my friends were in love, and—and I was loved by a lord's son!

I gazed in the direction of the forest and smiled. Could

it be that John had been the one all along? I stopped dancing.

"Sir, you are a lord, and I a peasant. This will never be." But even as I spoke, I put my hand slowly into my apron pocket.

The eye was not moving!

But wait . . . No, it did not move back and forth as if it were looking.

And yet it moved. It throbbed in my hand, and then I felt in horror that it squeezed out tears, so that in a moment my hand was wet with them.

I pulled my hand away and wiped it on my skirt, and I could not have been more repelled and appalled if it had been blood upon my hand.

John had been talking about his hopes for the king's understanding, and now he watched me, curious, expectant, and . . . lovingly.

"Sir—John, I must go home, I—I must think."

"Think and dream, Keturah, as I will," he said.

I ran away, up the hill toward home, my mind still dancing with disbelief.

I gazed out my window and watched the lanterns flicker and listened to the music and laughter that rose like field butterflies from the village. A fairy tale had happened to me—I was the told instead of the teller.

It was not long before Gretta and Beatrice appeared at my door. They regarded me in silent wonder for a time, and then Gretta said, "So the mystery of your true love is solved.

And he is John Temsland, a lord's son!"

"He is a beautiful man!" Beatrice exclaimed.

"He is," I said, smiling.

"And he is good and upright," Beatrice said. "And he is smitten with you, that is clear."

"So it seems."

"And he is a lord's son!" said Gretta again.

"Amazing," I said.

"Did he propose, Keturah?" Beatrice asked, smiling.

"He did," I said, half in wonder myself.

"And you answered?"

"I—I believe I forgot to answer."

Beatrice giggled, but Gretta stared at me. "Did you consult the charm?"

"It throbs and weeps," I said, "but it does not search."

"At last!" Beatrice said happily. "You are safe, Keturah!"

"But what does that mean?" Gretta asked. "Why does it weep?"

"I don't know," I said. "But I know this—fair day is a day of weddings. Now home with you, to dream of your loves. And let me dream of mine."

They left then, and I stayed awake the night through, trying to answer for myself Gretta's question.

# XIII

꧁ ꧂

*The king and the fair with its trappings
and delights; the cooking contest,
what I ask of the king.*

The day of the fair began with drums.

Drums beat in the village as traveling merchants from throughout the south of Angleland came to set up their booths and show their wares. Drums answered from a distance as the royal party came closer. The king was coming.

My friends came to my house early to wash their hair and don freshly washed frocks. They braided flowers into their hair. Grandmother was glad of heart and sang little songs as they made ready.

I did the chores slowly. I scrubbed and polished the pots as if it were the only important work in the world. While making the beds, I stopped to smell the scent of Grandmother on the quilt. I dusted the dear rocker and swept the familiar floor. I touched the life I had known and, as I now understood it, the life I loved. This I felt in my heart: tomorrow I would not be what I was today.

We all lined the streets to wait for the king and his entourage. At last, as morning became noon, the king rode into the village while heralds blew their horns and were answered by flutes.

The king came first, and at his right was the royal messenger, Duke Morland, who had told us of the king's intentions. At the king's other side was Lord Temsland. The astonishment upon his face was equal to the fury on the face of the duke. Mixed with the duke's anger was envy—it now appeared that when he and his cohorts had persuaded the king to banish Temsland to this corner of the kingdom, they had inadvertently rewarded him. The sun shone on the bay and the cottages dotted the hillside like flowers, and even the forest looked benign in the golden sunshine.

And then the bell began to ring and our hearts rose to see Lord Temsland's joy as he passed a hand over his eyes. John Temsland and his mother rode to greet the party and then joined it. As they passed us, John leaned over to hand me a red rose. The girls around me tittered and offered me quick curtseys when I looked at them. Truly I was safe, just as Beatrice had said. I smiled at the girls and smelled my rose.

We all cheered and showered the royal party with flower petals. The horses' hooves made a merry sound upon the new cobblestone road.

The lords who had come to gloat looked everywhere in dismay. Their countenances soured as they gazed upon our whitewashed cottages and the flowers that decorated every doorstep and pathway and gaily painted window box. They scowled at our cobblestone road and square, and stared morosely at our new pier and the gleaming bell in the church tower. They would not look into the faces of the people, so like flowers themselves in their bright clothes.

Tailor's children were brightest and prettiest of all.

The king and queen, on the other hand, beamed at our reception. Village girls walked before them, swirling long ribbons above their heads, and boys beat upon little tambourines. The king and his party slowed down when they came to the row of booths set up for the fair. Merchants bowed low as the king and queen passed.

Once they had passed they filed to the church, and Parson Tom welcomed them and all of us who had followed to the stairs of the chapel. Lord Temsland gave a speech.

"It is good to be home!" he announced with great good cheer. "If only I could tell you how *very* good it is to be home," he said, winking at us.

And then he became more sober. "And home it is indeed, I have learned. I have learned something else—that my son is ready to take on many of the responsibilities of a manored lord, and may well perform them better than I."

At this, the people laughed and clapped, and John blushed to be praised. Lord Temsland, too, flushed at the enthusiasm of everyone's agreement.

He continued, "I have learned that by opening the coffers, one obtains other treasures, and that . . ." He paused and looked about him. "Well, enough of speeches. Surely it is time for the fair to begin!"

This time the cheering was deafening.

Parson Tom raised his hand. "God bless this fair," he pronounced then. "Let the fair begin."

Someone began to play a pipe, and a few sang together.

I heard the king talking to Lord Temsland as a friend talks with another.

"Tomorrow we will hunt the great hart," Lord Temsland said to the king. "He has evaded me for many years now, and has grown into a noble animal. He is as intelligent as he is large, helping other deer escape from traps, leading them to our haystacks when it was bitterly cold last winter. My arrows have not been able to find him, but surely yours will, Your Majesty."

The king smiled and looked with longing toward the forest. "There is nothing I like more than a challenging hunt," he said.

John and I exchanged a look.

"The hart cannot be caught, Father," John said. "He is enchanted, perhaps. It would be better if we sought out a more likely target."

The king frowned. "No beast escapes my arrow, once my heart is in it," he said.

"Of course not!" Lord Temsland said, and then they both laughed, and the king put his hand on Lord Temsland's shoulder.

I watched Parson Tom slump in his chair and promptly go to sleep. His goiter was larger than usual. One day soon he would sleep and not awake, his goiter having sucked the life out of him.

But I did not want to see such things today. I wanted the noise and music and laughter of the fair, and so I took Grandmother's hand and plunged into the middle of it.

The morning began with a boulder pull. Everyone predicted that it would be Simon Langley or Barnaby Buttercross who would pull the boulder the farthest. Hadn't they won, one of them, every year for seven years? But weren't we all surprised when Stephen Little won the day. He lived in the rockiest part of the parish and had become good at taking rocks out of his poor soil. Lord Temsland was so pleased at the turn of events that he promised Stephen the right to clear another half-acre of forestland that bordered his portion.

When the boulder pull was ended, everyone went to see the booths of vegetables and goods. There were cabbages and rhubarb, corn, leeks and cucumbers, beans and garlic, and white meats of milk and cheeses. There were gooseberries and rye and wheat breads, baked and warm, golden butters in fancy molds, and bunches of picked flowers tied with ribbon. Martha Hornsby sold her famous jams and syrups, and Lord Temsland gave her a great gold coin for one bottle. This made her cry, for all her life she had longed to have a real gold coin to bite of an evening.

A number of youths entered the eating contest, and a great crowd gathered round and bet on who would be able to eat the most currant buns. Jeremy Smith ate until he was sick. Richard Walters had to stop at twenty, and then spent the better part of an hour lying on the village lawn, moaning. Michael Red ate thirty-three buns and stopped, saying that it was a lucky number and that it was the first time in his life he had been full. Michael's wife was very proud of him and wove his first-place blue ribbon into her hair.

The young lads were stoic when they all lost in archery to Barty Lumberjon. They knew he wouldn't let them forget his victory until next year's fair, but freedom from enforced humility came when Adam Wiltweather beat Barty in the arm-wrestling competition. Adam was a quiet lad who would let others win at times and declare he had done his best.

I walked Grandmother around the booths. We touched woolens and silks, tasted strange foods, smelled exotic spices. We saw a man juggle fiery torches, then raw eggs. Grandmother clapped with happiness to see a man who could tie himself into a knot. The villagers proudly showed their calves and bulls and their lambs and ewes and their turkeys and roosters and hogs. Children showed their prize rabbits and donkeys. Grandmother and I laughed and clapped, and I marveled to think it possible that I might be lady over all my people.

Then came the judging of fruits and vegetables. Ben Marshall won, of course, for melons and pumpkins and cabbages and turnips and leeks. The other fruit and vegetable ribbons were shared, one per person, and there was some debate over whether the winners' produce was truly better than Ben Marshall's. Biddy Sodwell's strawberries were bigger, but weren't Ben's sweeter? Sam Baxter's lettuces were larger, but weren't Ben's greener and crisper? Still, Ben was happy, and announced over raised mugs that he would marry Best Cook that very night while still in the glow of his triumph.

Soor Lily's great baby son won the wrestling contest

and gave the ribbon to his mother. Soor Lily herself did not enter any contest but sold many bottles of her "tonic," which cured everything from warts to melancholy. A man who had several warts on his nose drank an entire bottle, and within minutes every wart fell off. He was so happy he proposed to Soor Lily, and was immediately chased out of town by three of her sons.

Goody Thompson won a contest by guessing the correct number of beans in a jar and got a beautiful new teapot for her prize. She carried her baby as she walked about the fair; his cheeks were growing fat and rosy.

Gretta won a blue ribbon for some exquisite embroidery, but it was well known that her most important contribution was being worn by Lady Temsland, who was every bit as gorgeously arrayed as the queen.

There was one surprise in the textiles category. Master Tailor displayed a beautiful gown of lavender silk and won hands down, of course. As soon as he had been presented the ribbon, he gave the gown to Gretta. " 'Tis a wedding gown," he said. "And if I have any eye at all, it will fit you perfectly."

She held it up in a rapture, then looked at him sternly. "You must promise never to boss me."

Tailor smiled. "And if I tried?"

"Why, I would love you anyway," she said, smiling.

They embraced, and we all clapped to see it, none more loudly than Tailor's children.

Choirmaster's choir sang for the king and queen while they ate a dinner that sampled all the finest foods of the fair, including Cook's blue-ribbon loaves. The great lords who had accompanied the king now were friendly to Lord Temsland and cold to Duke Morland, who sat alone and glum, apart from the others. Apparently they had decided it was the duke who had exaggerated.

Now all that was left was the judging of Best Cook. I had entered my pie for the sake of Tobias, who had boasted that the queen would eat a dish made of his lemons. There seemed no need now to see the judging, but my friends took me by the hands and pulled me to the cookery tent. Along the way, we skipped and sang, bartered with the merchants, and cooed over babies.

Under the tent, the dignified panel of judges still tasted and conferred. They had placed a blue ribbon on Padmoh's teacake and a red on her bean soup. And so it was in every category except pies—the judges had yet to decide that category. My heart lifted at the sight of all Padmoh's ribbons. Of course she would win. Ben Marshall had eyes only for the judges.

Finally, one judge tasted my lemon pie. He moaned and sighed with pleasure.

Then the other judges tasted, and kept tasting more and more until the pie was half gone.

And then they placed a blue ribbon on the plate.

The head judge announced, "This one pie is so exquisite, so unusual, that we must declare Miss Keturah Reeve the Best Cook of the fair!"

My friends cheered and laughed, and the crowd gathered round to congratulate me. "It seems unfair that one pie should win me Best Cook when Padmoh won so many ribbons," I said. But my protest was taken for false modesty, and the judges begged for my lemon pie recipe.

Though Ben Marshall could not get close to me, he smiled and tried to catch my eye. "There is my bride," he said to some of those around him, and they raised a glass to his good fortune. I felt sick inside that I had given him false hope, and I took no joy in Padmoh's sad countenance.

Just as Ben was about to leap toward me out of the crowd, a horn sounded. Its call was long and sweet, a call to come to the square. The crowd moved as one in that direction, I in the middle. I saw that Ben fell farther back.

Again the horn sounded. Musicians began to play as we gathered in the square, and even the merchants and entertainers came away from their booths and stages and gathered to listen.

John Temsland caught me away from the crowd. "We have both won," he said.

"As well you should," I said. "You have done well. It made me glad to witness Duke Morland's unhappiness at not seeing your father humiliated."

"The king said I should have my wish granted," John said. "All is going as I planned."

"And what will you ask?"

"I asked him to give you whatever *you* would ask," said John. "It is for you to decide, Keturah. Father knows my heart. Ask to be made Lady Keturah Reeve, and before the hour is up, I will marry you."

And then he slipped away, and though the crowd closed in around me, I was alone with secret wonder.

The king was in full regalia and wore a crown of gold and rubies. The queen also was dressed in purple velvets and ermine, and wore a coronet of silver and diamonds. She was the only one not looking upon us. She was eating something, and only after several bites did I see it was a piece of my lemon pie.

"Come with us, closer to the king," Beatrice said, taking my hand. She was still dressed as a boy from singing in the choir. We pushed through the people to the front of the gathering.

There was a call of trumpets, and the musicians ceased to play and the people listened.

"I thank the people of Tide-by-Rood and Marshall for welcoming me to their beautiful lands," said the king.

The people cheered and whistled and threw their hats into the air.

"I have promised a shoe full of gold to the one who most delighted me at the fair. In the end, Lord Temsland had his choice, and his lady hers. I have my choice, and my queen hers. And so we will divide the gold four ways.

"First, Lord Temsland's choice. To the lead soprano of the choir, a quarter of a shoe of gold. Come forward, soprano."

Beatrice as Bill glanced nervously at us and then stepped forward.

I could not hear what she said, but Gretta and Choirmaster gasped when she did not bow but instead curtseyed. The king, however, only laughed, and Bill was invited to remove his cap and let his long braids fall. The crowd murmured and one could hear stifled laughter. At first Lord Temsland seemed somewhat flustered, but his wife's gentle amusement calmed him, and he was further calmed to see that the king was not disturbed by the disguise.

"Well, the bishop of Great Town has women in his choir," the king said. Turning then to Lord Temsland, he added, "And if you wish to be in style, you must not put your women in disguise."

"Your Majesty," Beatrice said, "if I may, it was my own deception. I beg your forgiveness."

Gently the king said, "How can I give you that? It would be like offering forgiveness to an angel. But I can give you this." He handed her a small velvet purse that jangled with gold. "And what would you have for your wish granted?" he asked.

"Your Majesty, only that I might share your gift with someone," she said.

"And who would that be?"

Beatrice fetched Choirmaster by the hand and led him before the king. "Your Majesty, here is the man who makes me sing, for his music is the music of angels. And—and we are to be married."

The crowd murmured, oohed, and tittered with surprise.

Choirmaster dabbed his nose with a sparkling white handkerchief.

"I assume this match is also according to your wishes, Choirmaster?" the king said.

"Your Majesty, it is," he said, bowing deeply before the king. He did not let go of Beatrice's hand.

"You must write an Easter mass for me next year," the king said, "for which I will pay you in gold."

"It has always been my deepest desire," Choirmaster said, smiling—the broadest smile I had ever seen upon him.

The couple backed away, and the king called, "Now the Tailor." Tailor came forward and I saw that he was wearing not even one item of orange clothing.

"You have done as fine a work as any of the royal tailors. You are Lady Temsland's choice," said the king. "Besides your gold, what is the reward that you would wish for?"

"To marry the woman who sewed most of the finery you speak of, Your Majesty," he said.

"Ah. And who would that be?"

Tailor gestured to Gretta, who came forward boldly and curtseyed.

"Is this your wish, young maid?" the king asked.

"Your Majesty," she said, "here is an imperfect man, the only one in the world perfect enough for me."

"Then it will be. And each year you will both come to my palace and sew my daughter a new Easter gown. For that I will pay you in gold."

"It has been my greatest wish," said Tailor, bowing with great dignity.

The villagers cheered, for there was nothing they liked more than weddings. The king raised his hand for silence.

"Keturah Reeve," he called. "Come forward."

I came forward and curtseyed.

"The queen has chosen your pie as the most wondrous thing of the fair," said the king. "You too will have a quarter of the shoe of gold."

He held it up to drop it into my hand, but I curtseyed again. "Please, I would ask that my share be divided among the poor of the village, Your Majesty," I said, for I knew that tomorrow I would not need money, that tomorrow I would not be what I was today.

The king turned and said a few words to Lord Temsland and John, and I turned to join the crowd.

"Wait, Keturah Reeve," said the king. "The gold will be distributed as you requested. But there is the matter of your wish granted."

I returned to my place before him.

John Temsland, beside the king, smiled and nodded at me, encouraging me. There he stood, so young and beautiful and strong, and he loved me. His mother and father, too, smiled gently, even lovingly, upon me.

I could ask now to be made a lady, and John would marry me. Oh, the good I could do for my people as the future Lady Temsland!

I realized that the crowd had been waiting for my answer. I waited too—waited for the words that would come to me as they always did around the common fire, waited for the words that would begin this new story of me . . . The villagers seemed puzzled by my silence, as if they all knew precisely what they would ask for me if it were up to them to choose. No one appeared more puzzled than John.

I knew I must speak, and I must speak now.

"Your Majesty," I said. He was a dear lad, John Temsland, so handsome, with hair the color of ripe wheat and eyes clear as a baby's, who loved me . . .

"Speak, Keturah," John said.

I felt the evening sunshine upon me—but what was the joy of sunshine if there were no night? Wasn't the sunset the sweetest time of day? Could I ask for only day and never dark?

And what of my friends? Could I ask for them ever to be at my side? Already I felt them moving past me, faster and faster, while I stayed still. And oh, the peace in that stillness.

What of riches and gold? What of lands and honors? But when I thought of these things there was a silence inside me—a hollowness. It fit ill, like the wrong ending to a good story.

Everyone was happy—old and young, rich and poor, male and female. But I could not touch their happiness, could not hold it. It was a dream and not real. What was real was the sense that in this life I had never quite been satisfied, had never long been at peace, had never loved or been fully loved as I longed to be. I could not name what was in me then, but I knew that the cure was not anywhere around me—not in Grandmother's and my friends' smiling faces, not in our shining little village, nor yet in any of the booths of the fair.

No, all I could think to ask for was my one true love, and this not even a king could give me. It was in that moment that everything became clear. "Your Majesty, I ask"—there was an audible intake of breath from the crowd—"I ask that the great hart and his mate no longer be hunted."

The king looked at me, astonished, and then at John. I did not look at John. I would not. I could not. Behind me the people were murmuring among themselves.

"Very well," the king said at last. "It is a strange thing you have asked, but you shall have it. Lord Temsland, John, do you swear?"

"We swear," John said after a brief silence, and in his voice was an accusation, and great pain.

"It is done," said Lord Temsland, and surely there was a hint of relief in his voice.

The king motioned for me to come closer and, when I did, said quietly so that few else could hear, "It is an unusual request, Keturah, from an unusual subject. Tell me what you say of this. As I traveled past Great Town, I saw villages emptied, fields unharvested, the grain stalks bent and rotting. I saw people hiding in holes like animals, and cattle dead by the roadside, and everywhere the smell of plague. But here, in Tide-by-Rood and Marshall, is health and marrow and wholesomeness. It is my understanding that it is because of you that this is so."

"No, Your Majesty, but because of one greater than I, and, forgive me, greater even than you."

He studied me then, a long moment, and nodded solemnly. "Tell him—tell him I have learned something. And thank him—or I suppose I shall myself one day."

The music began again at a nod from the king, and the villagers dispersed to their fairing. And I—I guessed that the shadows of the forest were beginning to touch my cottage, and I walked toward it.

❦

Gretta and Beatrice saw me leaving and broke away from their men and the friends and family who had gathered to congratulate them. Gretta grabbed my shoulders.

"Keturah!" she said. "Where are you going?"

"Home. I am tired."

Beatrice leaned her head against my shoulder. "Please don't leave, Keturah. You are so pale, you frighten me."

"Do not fret," I said, stroking Beatrice's hair. "Not today."

"Keturah," Gretta said, "promise us that you won't go into the forest."

"You have weddings to plan," I said. "Come, I will not be gone so long."

Then their families and lovers came laughing to steal them away, not understanding why Gretta had begun to weep, and I continued on.

# XIV

~⚜~

*A conclusion of sorts.*

I entered the cottage as the last rays of sunshine fell on swirling dust motes. I straightened Grandmother's bed, put away the bowls that had been left on the table, and went to Grandmother's chest and unwrapped my cornstalk doll. Gently I cradled her in my arms, remembering now that she had never had a name. After a time I put her carefully away, then walked through the garden to the forest.

How thin the air felt at the forest's edge, how ghostly the trees that guarded their realm. I looked around me. The whole world seemed as delicate as a dandelion seed, and as fleeting. Though the sun had not set, the moon had risen, and the village had never looked so beautiful. How sad to know that the figment village of my imagination would not vanish when I ended, to understand that it was not I who had invented the moon the first time I realized how lovely it was. To admit that it was not my breath that made the winds blow. It was not only my own life I mourned. Wouldn't all life end with mine? Reason told me it was not so, but my heart, my heart knew that when I closed my eyes I invented the night sky and the stars too. Wasn't the whole dome of the sky the same shape as the inside of my skull? Didn't I create the sun and the day when I raised my eyelids every morning?

No. As if I had suddenly grown up, my heart was schooled. My friends, my village, and Angleland would all go on. They had already left me behind.

I turned away from the village and stepped into the forest.

———⟨⟩———

In a little while I could no longer hear the familiar sounds of the village—the laughter of children, the squawks of geese, the lowing of cattle. All I could hear was the shushing of the green sea of leaves, silencing me.

I thought I understood the forest from the days when I was lost in it. Oh, proud trees, so tall and hard, I thought. You would not bend to make me feel less small. You would stand still and watch me die.

The forest was rampant, pathless, and full of shadows. The forest was death, and yet as I walked I began to see the secret life beneath every leaf. I heard eyes blinking, heard small hearts beating. I put one hand upon a tree. Even in the cool shadows, it was warm. I stood still, and as I stood I saw birds flit from branch to branch, squirrels run from their holes, and a rabbit lope around a tree. A butterfly lit on a bush, and a graceful doe stepped briefly into my vision in the deep of the forest. The wood leapt and swayed.

Then I saw the hart standing still as a tree trunk nearby in the shadows. He looked at me. Silently he turned, and just as silently I followed.

I followed the hart until I thought I had lost him. Then I found him, then lost him again. Soon I knew I was lost in the wood, and I sat against a tree. I daydreamed that my whole life until then was a story I had made up and now had forgotten, all but the end. It was a lovely gown I had tried on for a time, a gown whose color I could not now recall. It was a delicious meal that had not filled me.

The sound of a horse brought me to my feet. When I saw the black stallion approaching, I put my hand in my apron pocket. The eye was still as death, but I did not need the charm to understand the magic that was in my own heart.

Lord Death came close to me. I could feel no heat from him, hear no breath in his lungs. He was utterly still beside me, but there was a strange comfort in that stillness. It was as if he had eternity to stand beside me, and forever to listen. There was no time or motion to disturb us.

"And so there was no love for you?" he asked gently.

"Tell me what it is like to die," I answered.

He dismounted from his horse, looking at me strangely the whole while. "You experience something similar every day," he said softly. "It is as familiar to you as bread and butter."

"Yes," I said. "It is like every night when I fall asleep."

"No. It is like every morning when you wake up." He searched my face, touched it gently with fingers so cold they burned along my jaw, my temple, my lips, burned me to the very core. "But to know that is never enough. Keturah, I have abdicated my claim upon your soul. Come, I must take you home. Do you not know you have defeated me? That you have tricked my heart into loving you? Do what you will, marry whom you will, go where you will. You shall live to be a great age, and you shall not see me again until life has pressed its hand so heavily upon you that you wish to see it lift." He stepped away from me and offered me his hand to lift me to the saddle.

I realized that I held my life in my own arms, then. I cradled it, felt its warm weight and the breath of it. But I had come too far. I saw that the forest was more beautiful than the village even with its bright paint, that the forest's silence rang more lovely than Beatrice's singing.

I felt my life grow heavier in my arms until I could not hold it anymore.

I stood very tall. "Sir, here is my wish: that you take me to wife."

The breeze stilled, the birds stopped their song, and the trees seemed to bend and listen.

"You have determined you would marry for love," he said.

"I love you," I replied.

The trees breathed around us, sighing and singing and whispering. "Can I believe what you say?" Lord Death asked.

"I will tell you the end of the story," I said. "The very end, the truest end there ever was. Once there was a girl—"

"And such a girl," he murmured.

"—who, long before she was lost in the wood, loved Lord Death. Last year it snowed until June. She did not care, for love of him.

"When the hungry deer and their cold babies came

wandering into the town that blackthorn winter, she did not begrudge them her tulips, which they ate stem, stalk, and bud. She did not begrudge them all the yellow of her stolen spring. The hope of yellow must be nothing to the taste of it, she thought.

"In fall, she knew it was Death who sweetened the apples. He made her see the sun in a blue sky and hear the trees in a spring wind. He made her see how much she loved her friends, for all their trouble, and how much her grandmother loved her, and oh, he made her love the breath in her lungs.

"She knew she had never been truly alive until she met him, and never so happy and content with her lot until she was touched by the sorrow of him."

He lifted his hand as if he would take mine, and then he did not. "Keturah . . ." He dropped his arm.

"You, my lord, are the ending of all true stories."

I moved to touch him.

"I will not let you go with him," said a voice behind me.

"John!" I cried.

He burst from the bushes, vibrant life shaking the very air around him. His face was pale, his jaw set.

"I thought it was a fairy prince after all you were running away to, Keturah. I never thought—but it does not matter." John faced Lord Death. "Let her stay, sir. If you love her, you will let her stay, for I will make her a manored lady."

"John." I held up my hand. "John, stay back."

"In my realm, John Temsland, she would have the powers of a queen," Lord Death said.

John took a step toward him. His hands fisted up, then opened, then fisted again, as if they did not know how to fight such a foe. "I heard that you have a pirate heart, but I did not know until now how black it is," he said, his voice low and shaking.

"I love her," Lord Death said, and his endless eyes turned to me.

"If you love her, why would you take her to your dark dwelling? To your hell?"

Lord Death looked at John now, and there was pity in his eyes. "There is no hell, John Temsland. Each man, when he dies, sees the landscape of his own soul."

"I am not afraid of hell or of you!" John cried, taking another step closer.

And truly, Lord Death, in that moment, seemed to be nothing to fear, a dark and beautiful man only. The lightning went out of his eyes, and one shoulder shrugged. "Of course you are afraid of me," he said. "I can take the two things you value most—your life and your love."

John took another stride toward him, and I could hear the rage in that one step. He drew his hunting knife from its sheath. The wind lifted dust from the forest floor, filling my eyes with tears.

Lord Death raised one eyebrow. He drew his cloak aside a little, and the gloam multiplied out its folds. Night shied and whinnied.

"John," I said, my voice shaking, "will you kill Death?"

"No," John said to me, though his eyes remained upon Lord Death, "but if he takes you, I will follow." He turned his hunting knife backward, to point at his own heart.

I put my hand out to steady him, just as he had steadied the hart's mate that day in the woods that seemed so long ago. I felt my hand tremble, and with all the effort of my will I stilled it. "Don't you see, John, I must go with him."

The knife did not waver.

"John, I will try to tell you—" I kept my voice as even as I could, to calm him. "Doesn't Lord Death own my every breath? Doesn't thinking of him make me glad of a single day? John, I—I love him."

"How can you love Death?"

How could I explain that many times in my life Lord Death had walked with me, that he was inevitably a part of my life, my intimate, bargain or no, and that he had always been and must always be my companion, my soul-and-heart love. He had steadied me before—how many times? How many times had I thought I had escaped him, when truly it was that he had not yet claimed me? How often had I felt the power in his arms, power enough to change the course of a river, to bring down a mountain, to spin or stop the world?

At last I said, "His voice is cold at first, John. It seems unfeeling. But if you listen without fear, you find that when he speaks, the most ordinary words become poetry. When he stands close to you, your life becomes a song, a praise. When he touches you, your smallest talents become gold; the most ordinary loves break your heart with their beauty."

John turned his eyes away from Lord Death then, and

looked at me as if he had never known me. He blinked his eyes as if he were awakening from a bad dream. The knife point touched his heart.

"Stop him!" I commanded Lord Death.

"I cannot stop him. If he wants to follow you, he will. But—"

And then, though we did not hear him, we saw the hart step from the trees and into our small clearing.

He was so close we could see ourselves reflected in his great round eye. The muscles in his chest quivered to be so close to humans. John looked at him, his mouth agape. None of us moved for fear that he would bolt. It seemed that he looked at John as much as John looked at him.

"He makes you want to live," Lord Death said quietly to John.

John looked hatefully at Lord Death for the briefest of moments, and then at the knife he held in his hand.

Surely all the angels of heaven smiled when John's eye was drawn again to the hart. The hart took a step closer to him, and then slowly lowered his stately head to the ground as if he were bowing. When his head was completely lowered, he began to nibble at mushrooms.

John reached to touch the stag's antlers. His face forgot Lord Death, forgot me as well, and soon his right hand forgot to hold the knife and dropped it to the forest floor. Then Lord Death touched him, and John fell unconscious into his arms. Together we laid John comfortably on the ground. Lord Death nodded to the hart, who turned and stepped silently into the trees.

"He sleeps only," Lord Death said to me. "His father will find him soon, for the hart will lead him here. They will find you, too, and take you home."

"They will find my body," I said, "for I will go with you."

"You have no dower," he said. "Live, Keturah. Go home."

"But I do have a dower," I said plainly. "This is my dower, Lord Death: the crown of flowers I will never wear at my wedding." I could not stop the tears that filled my eyes.

He knelt on one knee before me.

"The little house I would have had of my own, to furnish and clean. That, too, is part of my dower."

"I will give you the world for your footstool," he said.

"And most precious of all, I give you the baby I will never hold in my arms."

Then he folded me in his arms and wept with me. At last I laid down my sadness, laid it on the forest floor, never to have it again. Together we mounted his tall black horse and rode into the endless forest.

# CODA

*Being a collection of endings, every one happy.*

Was it true, Naomi? Was it the end that must be?

But I am sure there are other endings that you would like to know.

Beatrice, for example. Beatrice sang in Choirmaster's choir, and in his heart, for many a long year. And though her voice was that of an angel, it was said by many that it was love of her husband that gave her wings. She bore many children, all of whom had her small nose and who became musicians in their own right. She died before her husband, who promptly went back to making the saddest of music and joined her in death not a long time later.

Gretta and Tailor moved to be near the king's court, where they bought a big house with a great door that Tailor painted blue. Gretta quickly forgot which were her children and which were Tailor's. Living to an extraordinary age, she mourned them all equally as she buried her husband and, one by one, her children. In this suffering she found the best sort of perfection—the kind that never demands it of others.

Ben married Padmoh after all, and while it cannot be said that they were happy together, it can be said that they both lived comfortably and fatly, and died just the way they wanted—of food. Every one of their four sons broke with Marshall tradition and married for love.

As for young John Temsland, he grew to be a great and beloved lord, and the king held him up to others as an example. John married the king's niece and loved her sweetly, and it is said he denied her nothing save her ongoing wish to hunt in the Temsland forest. That he was so adamant about this was a source of curiosity to her all their days, as was his wont to dream of a night and call out the name Keturah. But there were no other puzzles to him, and they were happy, as were their people.

As for Grandmother, when the fair was over, and when she came to know what I had done, she went into the garden and picked a large ripe strawberry, and then walked into the forest a long way.

"Oliver Howard Reeve," she called, standing there in the cool of the forest. "Oliver Howard Reeve!" she demanded again.

And soon, because I asked, Lord Death allowed her husband to come to her.

"Sybil," he said gently from the bending willows.

"You have all left me behind," Grandmother said, with the slightest hint of a sob in her voice.

"Ah," he said, "but someone has to be last."

And so they talked together of all the big and small things of life, and soon Grandmother's complaint became a thing of laughter, and she gave him the bright red strawberry and he gave her a lily-of-the-valley, and he took her hand and brought her through the woods to the meadows and the mountains. And oh, how we rejoiced over mountains together.

As for the hart—he lives to this day, as does the story of Keturah and Lord Death as it is told around the common fires of the great city of Tide-by-Rood.

THE END

# ACKNOWLEDGMENTS

Some books come quietly—they are intimately the writer's own, and even the editor need only touch it lightly before it is ready to be shared with readers.

Some, like this one, come with much help from others, and thanks are necessary. I wrote the first few pages of this book in a desperate attempt to fulfill a page quota while in my MFA program. My advisor at the time, Brock Cole, said, "There's a book in there. You should write it." When a writer of Mr. Cole's stature says you should do something, you are wise to comply. I'm glad I did.

I wish to thank M. T. Anderson and Jane Resh Thomas, who nursed along subsequent pages and encouraged me to see it through to the end.

I am very grateful to my typist and dear friend Valerie Battrum, without whom this book would still be sitting on my desk, a stack of hand-scribbled pages. She is always among my first and most valued readers. I am indebted also to Stephen Roxburgh, Katya Rice, and my daughter Sarah for their editorial expertise.

Thanks go to the Canada Council for the Arts and the Alberta Foundation for the Arts for their timely financial assistance.

Finally, I express my love to my youngest sister, Lorraine, who died many years ago of cystic fibrosis at the age of eleven. Now, as a mother and grandmother, I realize what a long journey dying must be for a child to make alone. I wish I could have walked with her a little way. This book is my way of doing so.